TEN-MINUTE TERRORS

TERRORS

CAMP FEAR & OTHER HIDEOUS HORRORS

By
Anne Bancroft Fowler

Interior illustrations by
Eric Angeloch

Lowell  House

BOOKS

ISBN: 1-56565-321-1

Library of Congress Catalog Card Number: 95-9468

Publisher: Jack Artenstein
Vice President/General Manager, Juvenile Division: Elizabeth Amos
Director of Publishing Services: Rena Copperman
Editorial Director: Brenda Pope-Ostrow
Project Editor: Barbara Schoichet
Art Director: Lisa-Theresa Lenthall
Typesetting: Laurie Young

Cover illustration by Laurel Long

Lowell House books can be purchased at special discounts when ordered in bulk for premiums and special sales. Contact Department JH at the following address:

Lowell House Juvenile
2029 Century Park East, Suite 3290
Los Angeles, CA 90067

Manufactured in the United States of America

10 9 8 7 6 5 4 3 2 1

CONTENTS

◊ ◊ ◊ ◊ ◊ ◊ ◊

To my grandchildren
—A. B. F.

To Christian, for his unflagging help
—E. A.

THE HORROR CLUB

Stacy's face looked bitter. "Here they come," she said. "The *cool* club."

Natalie looked over her shoulder. Talking loudly and laughing, a group of students swarmed confidently down the hall of Kennedy High School, bypassing Natalie and Stacy without a glance.

"How come they never speak to anybody?" Natalie asked.

"Don't take it personally," Stacy replied. "They think being in the Horror Club makes them special."

Natalie sighed. "It does," she said wistfully.

Stacy looked at her sharply. "Don't tell me *you* want to join?"

Natalie shrugged. "Why shouldn't I want to join?" she said, stepping aside to let Stacy get her books out of the locker they shared. "I mean, what's wrong with wanting to be popular?"

"Nothing," Stacy said, "if it doesn't mean getting scared to death."

Natalie frowned. "What do you mean?"

"I mean last year, during an initiation, the Horror Club

actually *did* scare a would-be member to death. They rigged up a haunted house that looked just a little too real, and it turned out the guy had a weak heart that nobody knew about."

"Wow!" gasped Natalie.

"Wow is right," said Stacy. "There was a big stink, and the school banned the club. But that didn't stop any of the members. Now they just meet off campus at each other's homes."

Natalie looked at her friend curiously. "How come you know so much about this club, anyway?" she asked.

"I used to belong," Stacy said in a monotone. "Brent, the guy who was scared to death, was my boyfriend." And with that, she turned and abruptly walked away.

Natalie watched Stacy walk away with mixed feelings. Now she understood why Stacy—probably the prettiest girl in the school—kept to herself so much. Still, in spite of what Stacy had told her, Natalie couldn't help feeling that she would jump at the chance to join the Horror Club . . . to be one of the "in" crowd. Besides, she'd just transferred to Kennedy High a month ago and needed new friends.

And so, right after doing her homework that night, Natalie decided to put together a plan of attack. She retrieved an old diary she had never written in and began to create a false history for herself, writing in it the scariest things she could think of. She dated the first entry two years earlier so it would appear that she had been keeping these records over a period of time. Nothing scary had actually ever happened to Natalie, of course, but she had a vivid imagination and wrote each incident with great personal detail.

When she finally fell into bed, exhausted and pleased

with her inventiveness, she had finished the diary and was thinking about her next step. Tomorrow she would make some careful inquiries at school. She was going to find out all she could about the Horror Club and every one of its members.

What she found out was that the club met off campus every Friday night. Natalie also learned that although there were originally thirteen members, the number now stood at eleven—six boys and five girls. She even had a class with one of the boys, Danny Archer.

Taking note of where the group usually sat during lunch, that week she began to hurry to the cafeteria at noon so she could position herself nearby. Then, after lunch, she would follow the members out into the school yard, hoping at least one of them would notice her. She did this for a full week, but nothing ever happened. As far as the Horror Club was concerned, no one in it even acknowledged Natalie's existence.

It was clear Natalie had to take more direct action. Danny sat right in front of her in English class. It was time to stop looking at the back of his neck and muster the nerve to talk to him.

One day before class had started, she tapped his right shoulder. "Uh, hi," she said weakly.

Danny looked around, said hi, then immediately faced front.

"I'm Natalie Arnold," she persisted.

"Nice to meet you," Danny said without turning around again.

Too shy to keep humiliating herself, Natalie was still determined to go on with her next course of action. When the final bell rang, she hurried from the class, letting her

7

newly written diary fall to the floor as she passed Danny's desk. Glancing over her shoulder from the door, she watched him pick it up. If all went as planned, Danny would read the diary and share it with the Horror Club. When they read all the frightening experiences she'd had, they were sure to ask her to join.

Sure enough, the very next day Danny turned to her and handed her the diary. "You dropped this," he said nonchalantly.

"Oh, thanks," Natalie said, taking the diary back. She was surprised that he had finished with it so fast . . . *if* he had even read it.

"Oh, by the way, there are some kids who want to meet you," Danny said, instantly erasing her fears. "Meet me outside the cafeteria at lunchtime and I'll introduce you."

Natalie nodded happily, sure she had died and gone to heaven.

◆ ◆ ◆

That lunch was one Natalie would never forget. It started off *so* well, the conversation was *so* cool, and Natalie was having *so* much fun. She couldn't believe how comfortable she felt with her newfound friends . . . and then one of the girls, Marcia, dropped the bombshell.

"I read your diary," Marcia said. "I hope you don't mind."

Natalie shook her head. "It's cool," she said, adding with a grin, "just don't tell my parents what I've been doing."

Marcia smiled back. "The only thing is, I had a little trouble believing some of the things you wrote in there. We *all* did."

8

Natalie frowned. "Really? Like what?"

"Well, the part where you actually contact this spirit," Marcia said sarcastically. "I mean, who are you trying to kid?"

There was a dead silence around the lunch table as eleven pairs of eyes stared at Natalie. "You don't believe it?" she finally managed to say in a strained voice. "Well, that's your problem."

"It is and it isn't," Marcia said. "You see, we have this club, and some of the members want you to join . . . but it's not for phonies."

Natalie looked outraged. "I'm not a phony," she said stiffly.

"All we want you to do is prove that you can contact a spirit," Marcia said. "That wouldn't be a problem for you, would it?"

"What do you mean, prove it?" Natalie asked, trying to stall.

"Come to my house this Friday night, make contact with someone who's dead, and you're in," Marcia said with a smug smile.

"I—I can't," Natalie said, beginning to regret the whole thing.

Marcia looked victorious. "I knew it," she told the others. "I bet she made up everything in that stupid diary just to get into our club."

Natalie gazed around the circle of contempt-filled eyes. "What I meant," she said to Marcia, her voice dripping with sugar, "is that I can't come to *your* house. You'll have to come to mine."

Danny looked relieved. "See, I told you she's okay." He smiled at Natalie. "We'll be there. What time?"

They arranged to meet at eight on Friday evening—which happened to be the thirteenth—and Natalie left the table in shock. *What have I done?* she thought frantically. *Friday is just two days away. How am I going to learn how to contact a spirit by then?*

Rummaging through her locker to get the books for her next class, Natalie tried to calm down. She was more than relieved when Stacy walked up, and she quickly blurted out her predicament.

"I don't know what to do," she concluded after telling Stacy every horrible detail. "I've got myself into a real mess."

"That's for sure," Stacy agreed. "Maybe if you tell them the truth they'll respect you for it."

"Not if Marcia can help it," Natalie said. "She's a real mean one."

"She's the meanest," Stacy mused. "Tell you what, maybe there *is* something we can do. Meet me here after school and we'll talk."

When they met after school, Stacy had come up with a plan. It wasn't perfect, but Natalie felt like it might work well enough to get her off the hook. Stacy's motivation, though, was to pull a fast one on the Horror Club. Eager to set the plan in motion, the two girls went directly to Natalie's house and got to work.

To throw her mother off, Natalie said that she wanted to have a "Friday the Thirteenth" party in the basement. She knew her mom would easily agree to that because she'd been worried about Natalie having to make new friends ever since they moved. In fact, her mom even offered to help.

"How about if you take care of the refreshments?"

Natalie suggested to her mother. "Stacy and I will get started right now setting up the basement." And with that, she and Stacy ran down the back stairs off the kitchen.

First they placed the Ping-Pong table in the center of the room and covered it with an old sheet. Then they set up thirteen folding chairs around the table—one for each member of the club, one for Natalie, and one for her "guest."

Next Natalie put a candle at one end of the table, where it provided just enough light to guide the club members to their places but was easy enough to blow out. The plan was to extinguish the candle the moment the spirit was supposed to arrive. Natalie would handle that part on her own while Stacy distracted everyone with loud thumping sounds. Then Natalie would begin to ask the ghostly presence questions, instructing it to answer with one thump for yes and two thumps for no.

It was Stacy's idea to call upon the spirit of the deceased club member, Brent. "Let the others ask some questions, too," she told Natalie. "That way they can't accuse you of setting it up. Since I knew Brent better than anyone, I'll be able to answer anything they ask."

◆ ◆ ◆

When Friday night came, the girls were ready. The basement looked just like any other as Natalie gave it one last check, but the girls had added something extra.

The house was old and had a separate boiler room housing the heating unit and pipes running along the basement ceiling to carry the heat to individual rooms. Luckily, it was still early fall and not cold enough to need heat yet, so Stacy was able to string lengths of fishing line attached to weights through the insides of the pipes. All the pieces of line ran out a vent into the boiler room, where Stacy would stay hidden, and when Stacy had to answer a question, she could do so by simply pulling on a string. The weight to which the string was attached would hit the inside of the pipe with a thump. That way the spirit's answers would come from different angles, making it appear that the spirit was moving around the room.

Natalie was growing increasingly nervous, and when the doorbell finally rang at eight o'clock sharp, she nearly jumped out of her skin.

"Relax," Stacy said as she headed for the boiler room to play her part in the charade. "Even if it doesn't work, we'll have some fun at the mighty Horror Club's expense."

Natalie grinned in agreement, then turned out the lights before she ran upstairs to greet her guests. Already the eleven members of the Horror Club were gathered in the family room, where her mother was serving them lemonade.

Seeing them sitting there so politely gave the whole scene a kind of normalcy that made Natalie feel like giggling. Instead, she put on her most solemn face and asked, "Are you fully prepared for what's about to take place?"

"What's about to take place, honey?" her mother asked.

Natalie's face turned bright red. "J-just the party, Mom," she stammered, trying to recover her cool. She turned to the others. "Come on. It's in the basement."

There was a little nervous laughter as everyone gulped down the lemonade, then filed out of the room behind Natalie. At the door to the basement, she stopped and looked at everyone. "I must caution you not to speak from this point on unless you are bidden to do so," she said, using the exact same words she and Stacy had decided upon earlier. Then she pulled a small flashlight from her pocket and, opening the door, preceded the group down the long flight of stairs.

Reaching the table, Natalie turned off the flashlight and lit the candle. Then she sat down and bid the others to do the same. Finally, with a lot of scraping and shuffling of chairs, twelve seats were occupied, leaving one empty seat between Natalie and Marcia.

"Please hold hands," Natalie instructed, "and close your eyes. You must concentrate fully on being open to the other world." She looked around the table, and seeing that everyone was cooperating, she took Danny's hand, then reached across the empty seat and took Marcia's.

For a moment, she let the silence settle in. Then she began to hum an odd little tune that Stacy said was one of Brent's favorites. As the song became identifiable, Natalie could feel Marcia's grip tighten and Danny's palm begin to sweat. Pleased with their reactions, Natalie took the plan to the next step.

"I'm getting something," she said. "Someone's trying to contact me." She paused as if listening and snuck a look around the room. In the dim light she could see the faces of the other participants. They looked frightened. *Serves them right,* she thought, then quickly closed her eyes again.

"If someone is there and wishes to speak through me, indicate by answering now," Natalie said. "Knock once if the answer is yes and twice if the answer is no."

There was a loud thump in response, and Marcia gripped her hand so hard that Natalie almost cried out in pain. Biting her lip to keep from laughing, she went on. "Do you wish to communicate with someone in this group?"

13

There was another loud thump.

"Are you someone known to this group?"

Again, a single thump echoed through the basement.

"If you wish me to reveal your name, communicate it to me."

There was a loud thump, followed by a period of silence, during which Natalie pretended to be listening to a voice only she could hear. "The spirit is spelling something," she announced to the others. Then she slowly spelled out, "B-R-E-N-T! Brent—is that your name?"

As Natalie spoke the name aloud, she could hear a collective gasp around the table, and she could feel Marcia's hand turn to ice. Suddenly a chill that seemed to rise from the very floor of the basement swept over Natalie, penetrating her flesh to the bone. At the same time the candle went out, pitching the room into blackness.

Marcia jumped up. Pulling away from Natalie, she overturned her chair and ran up the stairs into the light of the kitchen. The others followed, shrieking like frightened children. Then, when Natalie heard the brave members of the Horror Club run through the house, slamming the front door behind them, she burst out laughing.

"You can come out now!" she called to Stacy, who emerged from the boiler room with a whoop of joy. The two girls burst out laughing.

"You were wonderful!" Stacy exclaimed. "Even *I* got scared!"

"*Your* plan was the great part," Natalie said modestly. "They didn't even wait to ask questions. How did you get it to turn so cold?"

"I thought *you* did that," Stacy answered.

Natalie shrugged. "I didn't even blow out the candle."

Ignoring the unanswerable, the girls continued to revel in their victory. Then, after everything was cleaned up, Stacy headed for home.

"Thanks!" Natalie called after her. "I'm a shoo-in!" Then she added with a laugh, "But who wants to join a club of scaredy-cats?"

"*I'm* the one who should thank *you,*" Stacy returned. "This is the happiest I've felt since Brent's death."

Still reliving how she'd horrified the Horror Club, Natalie headed for bed. But as she started up the stairs, she saw a light coming from under the door to her room. *That's odd,* she thought. *I don't remember leaving a light on.* She quickly opened the door and was faced with a sight that completely stunned her. "Wh-who are you?" she finally managed to stammer, nearly beside herself with fear. "And wh-what do you want?"

There, seated on her bed, was the pale ghost of a boy, his eyes hollow, his clothes ragged and covered with dirt. He looked pitifully at Natalie. "You should know what I want," the boy answered in a puzzled tone. "*You're* the one who called me."

RAIN, RAIN, GO AWAY!

◇ ◇ ◇ ◇ ◇ ◇ ◇

Pausing before two crumbling stone pillars, the tour guide looked at the group. "You are standing on the Highway of the Dead located at the entrance to a Toltec city built around 750 A.D.," she said.

Thirteen-year-old Brian's eyes grew wide. "Cool!" he exclaimed, looking at the huge pyramids that rose out of the barren land beyond.

But Patrick, his twelve-year-old brother, just groaned. "This is more boring than the National Museum in Mexico City."

Their mother told them both to be quiet, and the tour guide continued. "In the foreground you see the Toltec pyramid of the sun, which is not as tall as those built by the Egyptians," she said. "Still, it covers more ground than any other known pyramid in the world. Nearby stands the temple of Tlaloc, the Toltec rain god, adopted by the Aztecs after they conquered the Toltec nation. From then on, when the Aztecs planted their crops, they held a festival in honor of Tlaloc to ask that he bless their crops with rain."

"I'd rather be watching the weather channel on TV," Patrick sneered, making Brian laugh.

17

"You boys are being rude," their mother whispered.

"Your mother's right," their father said. He pulled a wad of *pesos* from his pocket. "Go buy yourselves a cool drink. We'll come get you when the lecture is over."

The two boys bought their drinks from one of the vendor stands and were strolling toward the pyramids when they heard someone trying to get their attention. It was a young boy about their age, beckoning them to follow him. Instantly Patrick started in the boy's direction, but Brian grabbed him by the arm. "Are you crazy?" he whispered. "Who knows what he wants?"

"That's what I'm going to find out," Patrick said, pulling away and darting after the boy who had disappeared behind the stands.

Brian hesitated, not knowing whether to follow his brother or not. But before he could decide, Patrick reappeared.

"What did he want?" Brian asked.

"Tell you later," Patrick said. "Here come Mom and Dad."

The family explored the pyramids for an hour or more, and by the time they boarded the bus for their return to Mexico City, Brian had forgotten all about the incident. But later that night in their hotel room he found Patrick scrubbing a green stone in the sink.

"Look what I have," his brother boasted, handing Brian a piece of green serpentine carved in the likeness of a curled snake.

Brian held it up to the light. "Where'd you get this?"

"That boy we saw today sold it to me," Patrick replied. "He said it contains the spirit of that rain god, Tlaloc, and if I rub it, I can make it rain."

"Boy, are you stupid to fall for a story like that!" Brian hooted. "Where'd this kid get it, anyway?"

"He said he found it wedged between some rocks around the pyramids," Patrick responded angrily. "Now, give it back!"

Brian turned the stone over in his hand. One side had a row of symbols carved into it. "What's this etched on the back?"

Patrick took the stone and rubbed his fingers over the symbols. Suddenly a puff of smoke rose from the rock. Uncoiling like a snake, the smoke spiraled upward and formed a dark cloud over their heads. Then it thinned to an almost invisible thread of mist and disappeared into an air-conditioning vent.

"Totally awesome!" Patrick exclaimed, his mouth dropping open. "Let's see if it happens again."

"Are you nuts?" Brian cried. "Give me that thing!" Snatching the stone from Patrick's hand, he hurried to the nightstand and held it under the lamp.

"I've seen something like this before," Brian said, flipping through the book of Mexican artifacts his mother had given him.

"See. I told you," he said, pointing to a photograph of a stone carving that resembled a curled snake covered with brilliant green feathers.

Patrick read the caption beneath the picture. "'The rattlesnake played a great part in the Aztec culture, but the chief reptile is a serpent decorated with the tail feathers of the quetzal bird.'" He paused. "What's a quetzal bird?"

"How should I know?" Brian grabbed the book. "Let me read it. 'The Aztecs believed that snakes were connected to the rain god, Tlaloc. The origin of the pictured specimen

19

is unknown, but all evidence points to the Valley of Mexico.'" Brian closed the book and looked at his brother.

"So?" Patrick asked, a stubborn expression on his face.

"Figure it out, dope," Brian said. "The stone you found looks just like the one in this book. It's probably stolen. You'll have to return it to the Mexican government."

"No way! I paid five dollars for it," Patrick said. "Give it to me."

Brian held the stone out of his brother's reach. Although he was just a year older, he felt responsible for him. "Listen," he said urgently. "This thing could be a real artifact. You can't keep it."

"Why not?" Patrick insisted. "I could make lots of money with this rock—especially where they need rain, like in the Sahara desert."

Brian glared at Patrick. Once he got an idea into his head, there was no reasoning with him. "Look, tomorrow's the last day of our trip. Let me try to find out about the stone. If it is a relic—like the one in the picture—it goes to the museum."

"Okay, but you can't tell Mom or Dad. And you only have tomorrow. After that the stone goes home with me." Patrick grinned.

"For now, it's mine. So hand it over."

Reluctantly Brian passed him the stone. "Will you at least do me a favor?" he asked. "Put this someplace safe and don't touch it."

"Okay, okay," Patrick grumbled. Crossing to his bed, he stuck the stone under his pillow.

The two boys then went to bed, but Brian had trouble falling asleep. It had begun to drizzle, and the night had grown cold. He'd finally fallen into a fitful doze when

Patrick's voice broke into his sleep.

"Help!" Patrick cried. "I'm drowning!"

Brian flipped on the light. Patrick was thrashing about on his bed, obviously having a bad dream.

"Wake up," Brian said, gently shaking his brother. "You're having a nightmare."

But as Brian touched Patrick's shoulder, a thin wisp of dark smoke rose from the tangled bed covers and hovered over the boys. Alarmed, Brian jumped back. He rubbed his eyes, and when he looked again, the smoke had totally disappeared.

Patrick sat up. "What's going on?" he asked groggily.

"You tell me," Brian answered anxiously.

Patrick shivered. "I remember it all now," he said. "I dreamed I was swimming . . . but I couldn't breathe."

"I'm not surprised you dreamed about water," Brian said, pointing to the rain beating against the windowpane with a force that threatened to shatter the glass. "It's really coming down out there."

The boys talked for a few minutes longer, then Patrick fell asleep. But Brian wasn't so lucky. He lay awake for hours. He hadn't told Patrick about the smoke he'd seen earlier, and he was afraid it was going to reappear.

The next morning, after practically no sleep, Brian awoke to find the sky a dismal gray and the rain still falling in sheets. Crossing to the window, he looked down on the flooded streets below. A river of muddy water surged over the gutters and almost came up to the bumpers on the few cars on the street.

Later, when Brian and Patrick joined their parents for

breakfast, the tour guide walked into the restaurant with some disturbing news. "All roads are closed and tourists are advised to stay in their hotels," she said. "But such heavy rain is unusual in Mexico City. Don't worry—your flight is expected to depart tomorrow as planned."

After breakfast, Brian and Patrick went back up to their room to get a deck of cards. While there, Patrick saw Brian grab the stone from under his pillow. "What are you taking that for?" he asked. "There's no way you're going to leave this hotel to investigate it."

"You don't want anyone to find your precious rock when they clean the room, do you?" Brian countered. "Besides, I still might be able to find someone who can identify it." And with that, the two headed to the rec room in the hotel's lower level.

But the rec room was closed because the lower level floor was covered with an inch of water. Most of the shops down there were closed, too, but Brian saw a light on in the drugstore. Sloshing his way over to the door, he tapped on the glass.

A teenage girl came out from the back, hesitated, then crossed to the door and opened it a crack. "I'm sorry, we're not open today. I just came in to get something for my grandfather's cough." She spoke English without a trace of an accent and smiled at Brian's look of surprise. "I'm from California," she explained. "I came to spend the summer with my grandfather to learn about my Mexican heritage."

"Did you say Mexican heritage?" Brian asked. "Maybe you can help us." He pulled the serpentine stone from his pocket. "We were hoping to find someone who could tell us about this," he said, passing the stone through the crack in the door.

The girl turned the stone in her hands. "Sorry," she said. "I haven't a clue." Then the girl turned off the light, stepped out the door, and locked it behind her. "Come with me," she said, starting down the hall. "I know someone who may be able to help you."

She stopped by a metal door at the end of the hall and put a key into the lock. When the door opened, she stepped into a bubble-shaped glass elevator. "Come on in," she said. "The ride is awesome. You can see the whole city from here."

Brian and Patrick stepped in and the girl pushed the top button on the panel. Instantly the elevator began a rapid ascent up the exterior of the building.

"I saw this at night from the street," Patrick said. "It was all lit up. But our guide said hotel guests couldn't ride in it."

"It's my grandfather's private elevator," the girl explained. "My name's Pilar, by the way."

The boys introduced themselves, then Brian asked, "Does your grandfather own the drugstore?"

"He owns the whole hotel," Pilar explained with a shy smile.

The elevator slid to a stop and the silver doors opened. Pilar stepped from the elevator into a marble vestibule and the boys followed her, their footsteps echoing loudly on the polished floor.

The room beyond was large and elegantly furnished. An elderly man seated before a blazing fire looked up as the three teenagers entered. "There you are, Pilar," he said. "Did you have trouble with the alarm?"

"No, Papito," Pilar answered. "And I found the cough syrup you wanted. May I present Brian and Patrick Murphy, guests of the hotel. They need your help." She

23

turned to the boys. "This is my grandfather, Don Luis Romero. Show him your rock while I get a spoon for his medicine."

As Pilar left the room, Brian stepped forward and handed the stone to Pilar's grandfather. The old man looked at it closely, turning it over in his hand with an exclamation of surprise. Motioning the boys to sit, he rose and crossed to a wall of books. He selected one, returned to his chair, and opened to a page with several photographs on it. For a moment he compared one of the photographs to the stone, then he looked up. "This is very interesting," he said. "Please explain how this stone came into your possession."

"I bought it yesterday at the pyramids," Patrick offered.

"Do you know what the symbols mean?" Brian asked.

The old man nodded. "The symbols are a combination of pictures and written language that the Aztecs used to record various events," he said thoughtfully. "This particular phrase is an Aztec prayer to Tlaloc. It asks for rain."

"Does that mean the stone is real?" Patrick asked.

"I'd like to know more about it before I make that judgment," the old man responded. "You say you bought this at the pyramids? May I ask from whom?"

"Some boy," Patrick answered with a shrug. "I gave him five American dollars for it."

The old man smiled. "Well, there's your answer. If it were real the boy would surely have been able to sell it for more than that. I'm afraid it must be a fake, although a very good one."

"I don't care," Patrick said in a wounded tone. "I like it anyway." He put out his hand. "May I have it back, please?"

"Forgive me if I've offended you," the kind old man said, dropping the stone into Patrick's hand. "But you should be grateful the stone is a fake." He winked at Brian. "Because if it weren't, you would likely be Tlaloc's next victim. The god was said to be mischievous and would often answer prayers for rain by—"

But at that moment the old man's sentence was cut off by a great streak of lightning that lit up the dark gray sky beyond the window. A mighty peal of thunder followed, and both Patrick and Brian turned pale.

"Shame on you, Papito," Pilar said as she reentered the room and saw the boys' frightened faces. "What kind of stories are you telling our guests?"

The old man looked a bit sheepish. "I have just been trying to impress upon them the serious nature of the Aztec culture."

Brian rose. "Uh, we should go. Our parents will be wondering where we are."

"Don't take my grandfather too seriously," Pilar said as she led them back to the private elevator. "He loves to tell scary stories."

The boys stepped inside the glass-enclosed elevator, and as the doors closed behind them, Brian saw a huge flash of lightning hit the top floor of a nearby building. "Did you see that?" he cried, his voice nearly drowned out by a huge clap of thunder.

"I'm scared, Brian," Patrick said, taking the stone from his pocket as the elevator began its rapid descent. "That boy said this is real, and I believe him." He paused. "What if Tlaloc has decided to play a prank on us or something?"

"Don't be silly," Brian said. But just at that moment a flash of lightning crackled toward them from the eye of the

25

storm. The thunderbolt struck the glass elevator cab and both boys were thrown to the floor as they lurched to a stop.

"I can't see!" Patrick screamed, blinking his eyes.

"Hang on!" Brian yelled. Also blinded by the bright flash, he crawled across the floor until he felt the metal doors of the elevator. Then feeling his way to the control panel, he pushed the button. There was a click, but the elevator didn't move.

"We're stuck," Brian said, rubbing his eyes. As his sight returned, Brian could see Patrick curled on the floor of the elevator. "Patrick!" he called in alarm. "Are you all right!" He reached over and shook his brother, but Patrick only breathed raggedly.

"Help! Somebody, help!" he shouted, pounding the elevator buttons with his fist.

Outside, the rain continued to pour . . . and then an icy drop of water splashed on Brian's forehead. Panicked, he looked up at the ceiling and saw that water had collected in the overhead light fixture and was beginning to overflow.

Brian's heart began to pound. Water coming through the top of the elevator meant that the glass shaft itself was leaking from above. Soon the whole elevator car would be enveloped in water!

With a sob, Brian dropped to his knees beside his brother. Patrick was barely breathing now, his air intake hampered by a dark smoke that was rising from the stone in his hand.

Bolt after bolt of lightning illuminated the sky, followed by a terrible thunder that Brian could have sworn sounded like deep, evil laughter.

Frozen with fear, Brian watched the smoke spiral

upward from Patrick and drift toward him. He felt it brush his face, his lips, his nostrils. It was pleasant, like a summer breeze.

Maybe this won't be so bad, he told himself. It was the last thought he had before the smoke choked off his breath.

THE SECRET
OF THE SLIME

◊ ◊ ◊ ◊ ◊ ◊ ◊

David had stopped believing in his mom's favorite saying—"Be careful what you wish for, because it might come true"— a long time ago. In fact, he'd been wishing his little brother, Joshua, would miraculously vanish the minute his folks brought him home from the hospital. But six years later the little pest was still around, tailing him wherever he went.

But this Friday, David had decided, was going to be different. He was going to spend the evening in his tree house, exploring the heavens through his new telescope. And best of all, Laurel, the girl he'd liked all year, had agreed to meet him in the tree house to stargaze with him. He was sitting at his desk, reading one of his astronomy books, when his mom came to his room with his dad right behind her. Together they were going to change his life forever.

"Honey . . ." his mom began hesitantly. "Listen, Davy, sweetheart . . ."

"I'll tell him," his father interjected. "Son, I've got good news and bad news. I got a raise today, so your mom and I are going to the Crosbys' to celebrate. The bad news is you have to baby-sit Joshua."

"No!" David screamed, slamming his book shut. "I have plans."

"Now, Son," his father said. "Aren't you overreacting just a bit?"

David tried to calm down. "Sorry, Dad. I was going to use my new telescope tonight, and I—"

"Your mother's been cooped up in the house all week nursing Joshua's bronchitis," his father interrupted. "She needs a break, and in this family we help each other out."

"Well, I wish either Joshua or I would disappear from this family—*forever*," David muttered.

His mother heard him and her mouth closed in a tight line. David knew he had gone too far. "Well, until your wish comes true," she said sternly, "I'm afraid you'll have to baby-sit."

And so an hour later David found himself parked on Joshua's bed with the remains of a pepperoni pizza and a little brother to entertain.

"What'll we do?" Joshua asked, dangling a thick gob of cheese above his head and letting it swing like a pendulum over his mouth.

David shrugged. Then, looking at the melted cheese, he had an idea. "I know," he said. "Do you want to play with my Slime 'n Stuff?" It was the thing Joshua coveted most of anything David owned.

"Maybe," Joshua said suspiciously. "What do I have to do?"

"You can keep the whole jar," David replied, "*if* you stay alone for a few minutes while I set up my telescope in the tree house."

Joshua frowned. "But I want to go with you," he said with a pout.

David smiled. "You can't go outside. You're still sick."

"No," Joshua said firmly. "It's scary in the house by myself."

David could see that he needed a different approach. "Fine!" he shouted. "You're never going to touch *anything* of mine again." And with that he stomped down the hall into his own room. "Let me know if you change your mind!" he yelled, slamming his door and locking it. If he knew his brother, it wouldn't take Joshua long to follow.

Sure enough, it was only a few minutes before the sorry little guy was outside his door, coughing with the same hacking bark he'd had all week. David watched the doorknob jiggle for a second or two. Then, with a triumphant grin, David threw open his door and pretended to be surprised when Joshua flew into his room and planted himself on David's bed.

"Tell me a story, Davy," he whined, as if nothing had happened.

David thought fast. "If I tell you a story, will you stay in the house alone for fifteen minutes? Remember, I'll be right outside."

"Well . . ." Joshua paused. "Only if the story's a good one."

"Oh, it will be," David promised, casting his eyes about for likely material. When his eyes came to rest on his jar of Slime 'n Stuff, he announced, "The story is called 'How the Magician Got Swallowed by the Slime.'" Then he launched right in, knowing Laurel wasn't going to wait for him all night.

"Once upon a time, there was a boy named Joshua," David began, watching his brother grin as he heard his own name. David had to admit it was kind of cute the way

31

the little guy settled back into one of the pillows and practically shivered with anticipation. "And Joshua had a clever older brother named—"

"David!" shouted Joshua.

"Right," said David. "Anyway, David owned a very cool jar of slime. But this was no ordinary slime—*this* slime had a mind of its own. It had originally been taken from the Bottomless Bog by a powerful magician, who kept it trapped in a jar and forced it to do whatever he wanted."

"Like what?" Joshua asked, his eyes wide.

David smiled. "Well, sometimes he'd use the slime as a cloak of darkness, so he could slip through the night unseen. But more often, he made the slime devour people he didn't like." David lowered his voice to a near whisper. "But one night, the magician forgot to twist the lid back on the jar, and the slime got out and swallowed him!"

"Wow!" Joshua exclaimed.

David grinned. Even though he hated to admit it, he was a pretty good baby-sitter. "And so the slime slipped into the sewer," he went on, "and it spread until it was in sewers all across the nation. Then someone very smart, who knew what kids like to play with, discovered the slime, and without knowing its powers, that person put the slime into jars and sold it to toy stores everywhere. That's how David got it. And one day he actually discovered the ancient powers of the slime . . . but only by accident."

"Really, Davy? Did you really do that?" Joshua asked doubtfully.

"Not *me*," David said, pointing to himself. "The David in the story, remember?" He paused for effect. "Now, one night David was forced by his cruel parents to baby-sit his little brother. So he kindly decided to share the secret of the slime and teach Joshua how to use it."

"You will?" Joshua cried, wriggling with excitement.

David nodded. "I will if you don't tell Mom and Dad that I left you alone," he said. "Will you let me go outside and not tell them?"

Joshua nodded vigorously.

"Follow me," Davy said. He went into the bathroom with Joshua at his heels and dumped the glob of slime into the sink. "Now, here's what you do," he said, holding up the jar and pretending to read the instructions on the back. "Stir the slime around with your left hand, while you read all the words on this jar—backward. When you finish, the slime will come to life and its magical power will be yours to command."

"But I can't read," Joshua protested.

"Then just start from the end and say all the letters," David countered. And with that he backed out of the bathroom. "Remember," he said as Joshua began reciting the letters, "you can't skip a single letter. If you do, you have to start all over again."

"Okay!" Joshua said, his eyes glued to the jar.

"Whoops!" David yelped with a grin. "Now you have to start all over again." He hesitated at the door for a moment, and when he heard Joshua start over again, David stifled a chuckle and ran down the stairs, hoping that Laurel would still be waiting for him.

But by the time David got to the tree house, Laurel had come and gone, leaving him a note about meeting Monday in the cafeteria. Disappointed, David looked up at the sky. "Oh, well," he muttered. "At least the stars stuck around." He quickly set up his telescope and began to stargaze. A half hour later, he remembered Joshua.

Guiltily David glanced at the house. It seemed peaceful enough. *Everything's okay,* he thought with relief. *What am I worrying about, anyway? Josh would be screaming bloody murder if something were wrong.* And so David decided he could stay just a few minutes longer.

◆ ◆ ◆

When David next looked at his watch, almost two hours had passed. He scrambled down the ladder, and as he raced across the back lawn, he could see that the top floor of the house was dark while the ground floor was ablaze with lights. He grabbed the back doorknob and groaned out loud when he discovered that it was locked.

"Mom and Dad are going to kill me," he muttered as he ran around to the front of the house and rang the bell. That's when all the lights went out.

"The brat's playing games with me," he grumbled. And then he remembered the spare key under the back door mat. He rushed around the house again, grabbed the key, and jammed it into the lock. But when David pushed on the door, it wouldn't budge. *That's odd,* he thought. *It's cold out here, but this door is boiling hot.*

"Joshua?" David called, terrified that his brother had set the house on fire. He rapped sharply on the door, and as he did, he felt a tingle run through his hand, like an electrical shock. He leaned on the door. It was vibrating!

David jumped back. *What's going on?* his mind raced. "Joshua!" he screamed. "If you're trying to be funny, forget it! Now, let me in!"

Stopping to think, David decided to go in a window. He walked around the side of the house and tried the sliding glass door that opened onto the patio. But it, like every

34

other window within his reach, was locked. The curtains were all tightly drawn, too, their edges pressed together as if clutched by unseen hands. David watched from outside as they billowed in and out . . . like someone breathing.

"Davy?" Joshua suddenly called, followed by a little cough. "I'm down here."

David looked down. He could see Joshua's hand protruding, ghostlike, from between the bars of the opened basement window.

"What are you doing down there?" David squawked in alarm. "Mom and Dad will kill me if they find me outside and you in—"

"Shhh!" Joshua whispered. "Not so loud!"

As David bent down, he could smell an odor like rotten eggs. Holding his nose, he tried to breathe through his mouth. "What's going on down there, Josh?" he croaked.

Joshua's face was pale in the moonlight, his eyes round and staring, his cheeks streaked with tears. He gazed through the bars vacantly. "Why were you gone so long, Davy?" he asked pitifully.

"I lost track of time," David answered, his voice dripping with guilt. "Josh, can you try to tell me what's going on?"

"I'm not sure," the frightened boy whispered.

"And why are we whispering?" David asked.

"It can hear us," Joshua said, pointing behind him.

"*What* can hear us?" David asked, starting to panic.

"The monster," Joshua replied flatly.

"Get real!" David said angrily. And then he saw Joshua's face crumple. "Okay, okay," he said more gently. "Don't cry. Tell me what happened to the lights."

"*It* turned them out," Joshua said with a little sob.

"Okay, Josh," David said, trying not to sound annoyed. "Go get me the flashlight Dad keeps beside the fuse box."

Joshua nodded weakly, then slowly climbed down from his perch by the window and disappeared into the darkness. Meanwhile, David paced anxiously by the window until finally Joshua's little hand came through the bars to pass him the flashlight.

David quickly took the flashlight and directed the beam over Joshua's head, up the stairs leading to the kitchen. At the top he could see a puddle under the door that was oozing toward the steps.

David turned the flashlight on Joshua. "Is that what you're talking about?" he said, really annoyed now. "Go upstairs and open the back door so I can get in, right this minute. Whatever you've spilled, we have to get it cleaned up before Mom and Dad get home."

Joshua shook his head. "I can't go up there," he sobbed. "It's waiting for me. Please, Davy. Get me out of here."

"You're not making any sense," David said a bit more softly. "There's nothing waiting for you up there, Joshua. I promise. Now, be a big boy and let me in."

Joshua shook his head, wiping his nose with the back of his hand, and David stepped back to think. He knew it wasn't completely beyond his little brother to lock him out and make a mess. He also knew who would get in trouble for it. Pacing back and forth, David suddenly remembered that the attic had a window—a gabled window that he'd snuck out of late one night to catch a late movie with his buddies. Turning, he started toward the garage for a ladder.

"Where are you going?" Joshua howled.

"To save you from your monster," David replied.

A few minutes later David was pulling himself up onto the roof and scrambling over shingles toward the attic window. But when he cracked it open, he was almost knocked over by the foul odor that hit him in the face. It was the same disgusting smell that had come from the basement. Gagging and pinching his nose, David crawled into the attic and shined his flashlight beam around. It reflected off shiny patches of some kind of moisture on the walls. Reaching to touch a patch, David quickly pulled his hand back. It was a hot and sticky goo.

Suddenly he noticed something odd about the floor. It was vibrating—no, it was throbbing with a quiet but steady beat: *ba-boom, ba-boom, ba-boom*. It was a familiar rhythm, but one David couldn't quite identify. Then a strange warmth rose through the soles of his shoes. Pointing the flashlight downward, he saw a sticky ooze seeping through the floorboards, making dark puddles the consistency of half-melted Jell-O.

"What the—?" David gasped, lifting his shoe and seeing some kind of goop clinging to it. He didn't know what it was, but he did know one thing—he had to move quickly or get stuck.

Picking his way carefully through the attic junk, David crossed to the stairs that led down into the house. A strange light was shining from under the door at the bottom of the steps, and as he started down the stairs, the crack of light suddenly disappeared as if something had moved to block the space. That's when he became aware of the hum . . . a low-pitched hum, like electricity.

Holding his breath, David heard nothing except the constant *ba-boom, ba-boom, ba-boom* that had never stopped since he'd entered the house. He had definitely heard that sound before. But where?

And then, all at once, he realized where he'd heard that rhythmic pulse. It echoed in his chest—for it was the beating of his own heart, magnified a million times over.

Wiping a drop of sweat from his brow, David realized that the temperature in the house was rising, and each breath burned in his lungs. Now it didn't matter that his parents were going to be angry—Joshua was in trouble. The little guy had been right. Something was in the house. It had spread all over and was headed for the basement. Starting down the attic stairs more boldly now, his nerves under control, David was determined to save his little brother . . . until something warm fell on his shoulder.

Jumping, he pointed the flashlight overhead. There, hanging from the ceiling, was a thick oozing goo. Panicking, he waved the flashlight around and saw that the entire attic was now covered in the foul-smelling stuff. With no time to waste, he bounded down the few remaining steps and threw open the door, only to find a knee-deep sea of hideous, bilious slime flowing down the hallway from the bathroom.

"The slime!" David cried. Gagging from a stench worse than that of any sewer, he began to struggle back up the attic stairs, kicking at the ooze as he went. But it seemed to have a mind of its own and followed him, wrapping what felt like warm, clutching fingers around his ankles and tripping him as he tried to get away. With a sucking sound, the horrible slimy fingers lengthened and tightened their hold. Then a rush of slime surged down the stair from above, pulling him underneath it like warm waves of quicksand, filling his eyes, his ears, and his mouth.

As he fought for breath, clawing his way to the surface

of the slime, David could hear his parents drive up. Then he heard the car door slam and footsteps coming up the driveway. His parents were home! He needed to warn them of the danger.

"Look out!" he tried to yell, but all that came out were bubbles. Then, at that very moment, he sadly realized that his mother had been right—you *do* have to be careful what you wish for.

For as the slime slowly enveloped him—as he knew it had probably already done to his brother—David heard the last wish he had made ringing in his ears: *I wish either Joshua or I would disappear from this family—forever.* That awful wish, David now knew, was about to come true.

CAMP
FEAR

◇ ◇ ◇ ◇ ◇ ◇

Angela awoke with a start. There it was again—the same terrifying howl that had awakened her at midnight for the entire week she'd been at Camp Whispering Pines. Her heart pounding, she sat up and swung her bare feet out of her cot and onto the cracked wooden floor. Then she crept to the cabin's single window and looked out.

Kelly, her cabinmate, quietly snuck up behind her. "See anything?" she whispered.

Angela jumped. "Don't sneak up on me like that!" she snapped.

"What are you afraid of?" Kelly asked, snickering. "It's just the counselors trying to get us psyched up for tomorrow night." She turned away from Angela and climbed back into her cot. "I'm looking forward to Fright Night. Aren't you?"

Angela climbed back into her bunk. Kelly was right. The counselors were just trying to put an extra scare into them before tomorrow's camping trip. Nicknamed "Fright Night" because of some terrifying legend that the counselors told around the campfire, the trip was supposed to be the last test of each camper's courage before going home the next day.

"Angela?" Kelly's voice whispered in the darkness. "You're not too chicken to go to Fright Night, are you?"

Angela knew that Kelly thought she was a wimp and didn't belong at Whispering Pines, the elite survival camp that had come to be known as Camp Fear. And while it was true that Angela wasn't as athletic as some of the other kids, she wasn't about to be labeled a chicken. "No," Angela lied. "I can't wait for tomorrow night. It'll be a scream."

◆ ◆ ◆

The next morning Angela awoke to someone shaking her shoulder. She had dreamed of just about every imaginable monster and hadn't slept well. "Leave me alone," she grumbled. "I'm skipping breakfast."

"You already slept through it," Kelly said, still shaking her. "Now, hurry! Everyone is already packed and ready to head out. It's time to leave for the campout we talked about last night. You know, the one you're *not* too chicken to go on?"

Groaning, Angela sat up. "Boy, I sure don't see what's so great about being scared to death," she said.

"It's the reason we're all here, isn't it?" Kelly replied impatiently. "Come on, get up and pack your things."

Angela knew Kelly was right. The scare factor was what made Whispering Pines the most popular survival camp in the country. Located in a remote area of the Rocky Mountains, the purpose of the co-ed camp was to prepare teens for life by making them face their fears *and* overcome them. It had been tough on Angela, but she knew she had learned a lot more than Kelly gave her credit for.

"Well?" Kelly rolled her eyes. "Are you coming, or do I tell the others you chickened out?"

"I'm coming," Angela said with a heavy sigh. Then she quickly got ready and headed outside to join the group of waiting campers, prepared to conquer the last scare Camp Fear had to offer.

◇ ◇ ◇

The day was warm, and as Angela trudged along, she looked around at her fellow campers, all of whom seemed eager to get to the campsite and hear the legend that would test their courage. *They probably didn't dream of monsters all night,* Angela thought wearily. *Why did I come to this stupid camp, anyway?*

At noon the group stopped to picnic. Exhausted, Angela pulled out a small mirror from her backpack and examined her forehead. About a mile back, someone had let a pine branch snap back and it had whacked her in the head. It had hurt, and she was worried about the large red welt that was rising on her forehead.

"What happened to you?" Jan, one of the two counselors on the hike, asked. She ran her fingers over Angela's injury. "Hey, Bob," she called to the other counselor. "Take a look at this."

Bob trotted over, examined Angela's head, then looked at Jan. "She's fine," he said, then paused. "Besides, we need her." Then he threw Jan a wink and the two stifled a laugh, as though they shared some kind of secret.

Angela was about to ask what Bob had meant by needing her when Kelly walked over. "I think Angela's just trying to get out of Fright Night," Kelly offered smugly. "If you ask me, *I* think she's a chicken."

"I am not!" Angela shouted.

The two counselors smiled at each other and then at Angela. "Good," Bob said, throwing an arm around her shoulders. Then he turned to the rest of the group. "Let's finish our lunch break and get going. The campsite is still about two miles from here."

By late afternoon the group had penetrated deep into the forest, and finally the two counselors announced that they had reached their destination. Helping to pitch camp made the cut on Angela's forehead throb, but she wasn't about to complain. Instead, she quietly went over to the first aid kit to get some aspirin. That's when she overheard Jan and Bob talking about her.

"We have to be more careful not to let any of them get hurt," Bob was saying. "We need twenty-four. No more, no less, or else we can't pull off the scare."

"So we'll just keep an eye on her," Jan agreed. "It's only a little cut, but she was late in getting ready this morning. Do you think she'll chicken out?"

Bob chuckled. "No way! Didn't you see the way she reacted when Kelly goaded her?" Then they both burst out laughing. "She'll probably be the first one to fall for that corny legend."

Angela couldn't believe it. The counselors were laughing at her! But why? Had Kelly managed to convince them that she couldn't pass the final test? Well, she'd show them! She wouldn't even flinch when she heard that stupid legend around the campfire tonight.

But several hours later, after everyone had stuffed themselves with hot dogs, sodas, and roasted marshmallows and had settled down to listen to the legend, Angela felt a trickle of fear run down her spine. Unable to stop herself, she shivered unconsciously.

"Are you cold?" Kelly asked her with a sneer. "Or just chicken?"

Several people laughed, and Angela felt her face turn red. She quickly looked at Bob and Jan. "Go ahead," she said, defiance in her voice. "Scare me!"

Bob gave Angela a thumbs-up, then solemnly began.

"Long ago, a hideous monster lived deep in this very forest. It had the yellow eyes of a tiger and the forked tongue of a snake, and no one dared enter the woods for fear of being torn to shreds by its razor-sharp teeth." The counselor grinned evilly, baring his own teeth, and growled. After a ripple of nervous laughter spread through the group, he went on.

"Anyway, back in those times, simple hill folk lived in two towns on either side of the forest, and because they wanted to avoid the monster, they always made the extra-long trek around the woods whenever they wanted to visit each other. Well, one day the village leaders decided to bargain with the creature. They left a note at the edge of the woods asking for safe passage in exchange for half of their annual wealth. That included anything the townspeople grew, made, or hunted, which was—"

"Oh, sure," Kelly scoffed. "Like the monster could really read!"

Bob nodded. "In fact, it could write, too. And much to the townspeoples' joy, the monster left a note that said it accepted the deal. So every year the residents of both towns took half of their annual production to a designated spot in the forest . . ."— Bob glanced over his shoulder— ". . . which was somewhere right around here."

Angela squirmed uncomfortably as the counselor went on with the story.

"Now, this arrangement worked very well until after several years, when the towns' leaders forgot how frightened they had once been and began to resent the agreement they had made. 'Why should we continue to share with a monster who is old and feeble by now and probably can't take revenge on us?' they asked one another.

"So the next time the annual offering was due, the townsfolk set aside only one-fourth of their production for the monster instead of a full half, along with a note explaining that it had been a bad year. When the monster took no revenge on either town, everyone boasted of their cleverness, and the following year, they left even less."

Bob stopped for a moment. He nodded to Jan, who looked each camper in the eye, then took over where Bob had left off.

"Now, this sly monster was no ordinary creature," the female counselor warned. "It had two characteristics that set it apart from all the other monsters of the world. First, it understood human nature very well; and second, it was able to change its shape."

Everyone gasped with delight. Only Angela gasped in terror, but she quickly recovered by pretending she had to cough.

Jan smiled, waited for Angela to finish her fake coughing attack, then went on. "Well, the monster had been very tolerant—even understanding—the first year that the townspeople cut back on their offerings. But the second year, when the citizens brought the monster practically nothing at all, it decided to investigate. It disguised itself as a wealthy merchant and pretended to be interested in opening a business that would bring revenue to both towns.

"'But I do need to make a profit,' the monster told the towns' leaders. 'Do the people of your two towns have sufficient wealth to spend freely on the goods I am proposing to make?'

"'Have no fear,' the councilmen said. 'Our people are wealthy and our production grows larger every year.'

"Now, when the monster heard that, it became furious. Tearing off its disguise, it revealed itself to the council and bellowed, 'You will pay for your deceit! You may keep the goods on which you place such value. Instead, one night every summer, from now until the end of time, you will bring me two dozen children from the village of Whispering Pines!'

"Naturally, the townspeople begged the monster to reconsider. They promised to send their children into the forest to spend the night, but they asked the beast to allow the children to return to their homes the following morning.

"The monster thought this over, then agreed to spare any child who proved to be brave and worthy—*unlike* the leaders of the town. 'But,' the monster added. 'Children who merely *pretend* to be brave are simply liars in disguise. To them I will show no mercy!'

"And from that day forth, the monster's terrible cry could be heard echoing through the forest at midnight, reminding the villagers of their promise."

The counselor paused dramatically to look around the circle of wide-eyed kids. "And that is the purpose of this camp. To prepare two dozen youths to defend the name of Whispering Pines. You must answer the monster's call and prove that the town is worthy enough of being spared. Are you up to it?"

47

Everyone cheered. "Yes!" they shouted in unison. "We're ready!"

Only Angela sat in stunned silence. "But—but we're not from Whispering Pines," she stammered.

Everyone turned to look at her.

"Get a life, Angela," Kelly said. "You don't really believe all that stuff about a monster, do you? This is just a test of our bravery."

"But what about that horrible howling sound we heard last night?" Angela asked. She looked at Bob and Jan. "It was just you two trying to scare us, right?"

But the two counselors just looked at each other and shrugged. "Well, this Fright Night does happen to mark the thirteenth year of Camp Fear's existence," Bob said. "If the legend of the monster is false, tonight would be the night it could come true." He turned to Jan and raised his eyebrows. "What do you think, Jan?"

"Bob's right," Jan agreed. "Tonight would be the night."

Angela looked around the campfire at the circle of faces. She had no choice. "Okay," she said to the counselors. "What do we have to do?"

Jan looked at her watch. "It's eleven o'clock now. The first rule is that you must wait until midnight to start out and you must make it back to the main lodge at Camp Fear before dawn. The fastest time to date is four hours flat, in case you're interested in setting a new record." She grinned at Bob.

"Now, rule number two is that you can't try to take shelter from the monster," Bob said. "You must stay out in the open." He looked at everyone gravely. "Now, rule number three is extremely important. You have to stick

49

together. If you don't the safety of the whole group could be jeopardized."

With that, Jan and Bob got up, put on their packs, and headed off. "We'll see you back at the main lodge," Jan said over her shoulder. "Good luck!"

Kelly waited for the counselors to get out of sight, then she turned to the others. "Well, what are we waiting for? Let's get going."

"Wait," Angela said. "It's not midnight yet."

"Who'll know the difference?" one of the other girls jeered.

"Th-the monster," Angela answered with a shiver.

Two of the boys burst out laughing. "Kelly's right," one of them said. "If we get a head start, we might set a new record."

"But the rules—" Angela began, but Kelly turned on her angrily.

"Look, the rules are as bogus as the legend," she snarled. "Now, you can come with the group or stay here on your own." And with that Kelly started off into the woods. The others followed, and seeing no other choice, Angela reluctantly brought up the rear.

About a half hour later the twenty-four campers were well into the forest. They were moving pretty fast, and Angela was having trouble keeping up. Suddenly a blast of wind raced through the pines and whipped a branch across her arm.

"Ouch!" she cried. Then, looking down, she saw that the pine needles had gashed her forearm, leaving a row of long marks across her skin. The blood oozing from the wound looked black and shiny in the moonlight, and the sight of it made Angela feel ill.

Maybe Kelly's right, she thought. *I am a wimp!* Sinking to the ground, she buried her head between her knees until the nausea passed. When she looked up again, no one was in sight. The others had left her behind. Frantically looking at her watch, Angela saw that it was exactly midnight. As if on cue the same terrifying howl she'd heard every night at that time echoed through the forest.

The monster! Angela's mind screamed.

Scrambling to her feet, she fled into the woods in the direction she thought the group had gone and thankfully came upon them just a few yards ahead where they had stopped in front of a cottage. It was surrounded by a white picket fence and had a red carpet that led up to the porch. Two bright lights shone from windows on either side of the door, making the cottage look cozy and very inviting.

"Wait, everyone!" Angela called, stumbling toward the others as she saw them preparing to enter the cottage. "The cottage—it could be a trick! Remember rule number two— we're not supposed to try to take shelter!"

"Ignore her!" Kelly shouted to the group. "You heard the monster howling—it's in the woods! Get into the cottage. We'll be safe there!"

"No!" Angela screamed. But she was too late. Already her fellow campers were pushing and shoving their way into the cottage.

Terrified, Angela stood rooted to the spot and watched as, within seconds, the friendly looking cottage transformed into a terrible beast. First it began to rock as if struck by an earthquake. Next the welcoming red carpet turned into a terrible forked tongue. And finally the yellow lights in the windows became two enormous eyes, as the white picket fence turned into a set of razor-sharp teeth.

Screaming hysterically, Angela watched in horror as the cries of terror coming from within the cottage slowly died down. Then, to her astonishment, the cottage disappeared altogether, and the forest fell silent . . . except for another hideous howl that loomed up from behind her.

Trembling uncontrollably, Angela slowly turned around to face her worst fear . . . but she saw nothing.

"I beat you!" she yelled. "I'm the bravest kid that ever—"

And then her heart stopped as she heard a voice bellow out of the forest: "That was only twenty-three! The agreement called for twenty-four!"

Holding her breath, Angela swallowed hard. Maybe if she didn't move the monster wouldn't see her. But then she knew there was no chance of that when she heard the very last words she would ever hear: "Ah," said the monster. "There you are!"

HEART OF STONE

◇ ◇ ◇ ◇ ◇ ◇ ◇

Master Sergeant Harold Stone, U.S. Marine Corps, pulled the jeep to a stop and shut off the motor. "Wake up, Joel," he said, shaking his stepson awake.

Joel opened one eye. The sky was overcast, and pools of mist clung to the ground. All he did was groan.

Harry opened his door and got out. Walking around to the back of the jeep, he lifted the rear hatch, letting in a blast of cold, damp air. "Out!" he ordered.

"What time is it?" Joel asked, rubbing his eyes.

"Five-thirty. Hit the deck, mister." Harry strapped a backpack on over his fatigues and held one out to Joel.

Joel took the backpack reluctantly, climbed out of the jeep, and stood beside it, looking around in the early morning light. Harry had parked by the edge of a forest, but in the distance Joel could see the deserted slopes of the Mammoth ski area in Northern California.

It was late May—too late for skiers and too early for summer vacationers. The jeep was the only vehicle in sight. A nearby sign read "Inyo National Forest," and an arrow below pointed the way through the woods to the Devil's Postpile Ranger Station.

It had begun to drizzle, and Joel shivered, pulling his jacket hood over his head and groaning again. He knew it promised to be a dismal day in more ways than one.

Bareheaded, Harry looked skyward. "A little water never hurt anybody," he said. "Like I've been telling your mother, you need to toughen up." Slinging a thirty-foot safety rope over his shoulder, he turned to his stepson impatiently. "Move it, Joel. We've got a long walk ahead of us."

Joel sighed. "Where'd you say we're going?" he asked.

"The Devil's Postpile," Harry answered. "It's volcanic rock that formed thousands of years ago into columns that look like gigantic posts." He strode briskly into the forest, following the trail toward the ranger station. "Now, save your breath. You'll need it at this altitude."

I should have never let Mom talk me into this, Joel thought, trotting after him.

The two traveled in silence until the path ended and they emerged into a clearing where they found the ranger's shack. "You just caught me," she said, coming out the door, looking surprised. "We don't get many people here this time of year. You're not thinking about heading into the Devil's Postpile, are you?"

"Yeah, we are," Harry said. "Is there a problem?"

"I need to warn you that the trail may have been made unsafe by all the recent earthquake activity in the area," the ranger said. She pointed toward a stand of pine trees. "You really don't have to go up there. You can see the Postpile from here."

Joel looked to where the ranger pointed and saw a wall of rock columns about a half mile away, its ridge covered by low-lying clouds.

"The wall of the Devil's Postpile rises sixty feet, and some of the rock is crumbling from natural erosion," the ranger went on. "But with all the seismic activity we had during the winter, I wouldn't recommend hiking up there."

"You have earthquakes here, too?" Joel asked, looking around anxiously. "I—I've had just about enough of them."

Joel and his mom used to live in Southern California, near the epicenter of the big quake that struck the San Fernando Valley in 1994. It was not an experience Joel wanted to repeat. Luckily, after his mom married Harry, they moved to Oregon. Moving away from what Joel called "Earthquake Valley" was the only thing he'd found positive about his mother's marriage to Harry Stone—a man who treated him more like a recruit than a stepson.

The ranger smiled warmly at Joel. "I see you've got a healthy fear of shakers," she said. "Well, we've only had a couple of minor shocks around here. No more than 3.5 on the Richter scale." She paused for a moment, then looked at Harry. "Look, if you and your boy here are good hikers, I'd say you could make it. But I'd be careful." She got into her truck. "I've got rounds to make. Have fun."

"Thanks," Harry said. "I've been here before, but we'll be extra careful."

"Fine," the ranger said. Fishing around in her glove compartment, she came out with a receipt book. "In that case, I need to collect a seven dollar park fee from you."

"Seven bucks," Harry grumbled, reaching for his wallet. "What if we'd missed you?"

The ranger smiled and took the money. "Well, I guess you wouldn't have paid," she said, handing Harry a receipt. "This must be your lucky day!"

The ranger started her truck, then leaned out the window.

"Just one more thing," she said as she started to drive off. "The wildlife up around the Postpile has all but disappeared lately. Probably doesn't mean a thing, but animals do have a sense about things, you know. Anyway, if you see anything unusual, I'd leave if I were you."

Joel looked after the departing truck nervously. "Maybe we should hike someplace else. What if the animals are sensing an earthquake?"

"Listen, mister, you've got to stop using earthquakes as an excuse," Harry said. "Your mom and I talked about it and we think you need to overcome your fears."

"That's easy for you to say," Joel grumbled. "You weren't there."

"Maybe not, but I know it'd take more than an earthquake to scare me," his stepdad said. "Harry Stone didn't get the nickname 'Heart of Stone' in the Marine Corps for nothing." And with that he turned on his heels and marched rapidly into the woods.

It had quit raining by the time the two reached the base of the rock formation known as the Devil's Postpile. Joel had to admit it was pretty cool as he stared at the postlike trunks of stone. Some stood upright or leaned at odd angles, while others appeared to have been gathered by a giant hand and thrown around like pickup sticks. The sheer rock wall of stone posts towered over the area like a dark sentinel. Mesmerized by the ominous towers of volcanic rock, Joel shuddered. With its head hidden in the clouds and a white vapor rising from around its base, the Devil's Postpile definitely gave off an eerie feeling.

"That's weird," Joel said, looking at the ground. A steamlike mist was rising from the rocks beneath his feet as well. Kneeling, he touched one of the rocks. "Hey, Harry.

This rock feels awfully warm. How can that be? The sun has been hidden behind clouds all day."

Harry shrugged, then grinned. "Well, they say the Devil's Postpile is a tourist hot spot!" he said with a laugh.

Joel rolled his eyes. "I'm serious, Harry."

"I'm serious, too," Harry said. "I'm serious about not letting you let your fears consume you. Now, let's keep hiking, shall we?" Turning, he started off at an even quicker pace than before, picking his way over and around the log-shaped rocks with ease.

His curiosity aroused, Joel followed at a much slower pace. Clearly the evaporation of rainwater on the heated surface of the rocks was what caused the steamy effect. But what made the rocks hot? Closely studying the ground beneath his feet, he stopped at intervals to feel the surface of the rock. It was warm all over, but some places seemed hotter than others. In fact, at one point when Joel tripped and put his hand onto a large boulder to steady himself, he actually got scorched.

"Ouch!" he yelped, shaking his hand to cool it off.

"What the heck's the matter now?" Harry snapped.

"I'm telling you, Harry," Joel said. "There *is* something weird about this place. Feel this rock."

"I'm not feeling any rocks," Harry said flatly. "And I don't want to hear any excuses from you. We're going up to the top or my nickname isn't Heart of Stone!"

Boy, does that name ever fit, Joel thought. Then he yelled aloud to Harry, "I'm not making up an excuse! There's really something strange going on here, and I think we should leave. You heard what the ranger said about the animals. I think they left because they know something's going to happen."

57

"Listen," Harry replied sternly, "I told your mother I'd take you for a mountain hike, and that's exactly what I'm going to do." He took the rope from his shoulder and quickly tied one end around his waist. "Tie this around your waist. I'm going to make sure you keep up with me."

Joel sighed and did as he was told. There was no arguing with Heart of Stone Harry. "How long are we going to have to hike like this?" he asked.

"Until we get to the top," Harry replied. Then he turned, gave the rope a pull, and started up the trail, dragging Joel behind him like a cowboy with a roped steer.

"Wait!" Joel protested, stumbling along in the increasingly growing mist. "Can't we talk about this?"

But Harry didn't answer. In minutes he had already gone the distance of the rope, and Joel couldn't even see him in the mist. It was like walking inside a thick cloud.

"Hey, come on, Harry! Slow down!" Joel protested. "I can't walk or even see—"

But Joel's sentence was cut short when Harry let out a deafening scream. Then, in the same moment, the rope around Joel's waist jerked with such force that it brought him to his knees, gasping in pain.

"Harry!" Joel called. "Are you all right?"

There was no answer.

Frightened, Joel scrambled to his feet and began pulling on the rope that was now completely slack. When there was no more rope to pull on, Joel found himself holding nothing but a frayed end.

"Harry?" he called, his voice hollow as he staggered blindly ahead in a mist so thick he couldn't see two feet in front of him. "Where are you? Are you okay?"

Once again Harry didn't answer, and Joel started to

fear the worst. Either Harry was injured or he was playing tricks on him, waiting to spring out of the mist and scare him half to death.

His heart pounding, Joel froze and strained to hear Harry's footsteps, but the only sound he heard was the chatter of his own teeth. Then suddenly the trail ended, and squinting through the mist, Joel saw a huge gash in the earth . . . too late.

Stumbling into the opening and turning his ankle, Joel was unable to catch himself before he slid into the large crevice, banging his head hard against the rock. Instantly brilliant stars danced before his eyes . . . and then everything went black.

◆ ◆ ◆

When he came to, Joel was lying on the floor of an underground cavern. A misty vapor rose from holes in the rock floor, warming the air around him. Groaning, he sat up and sniffed the air. Something smelled like rotten eggs.

Sulfur, Joel thought. *I have to get out of here. But how?*

Looking up, he could see light shining down through the crevice where he had fallen. It was only a few yards above him, and the angle of the incline didn't seem too steep. Joel figured he could climb out. At least he knew he had to try.

Struggling to his feet, Joel grimaced from the pain in his ankle. Then resolving to save himself, he started to climb when he heard his name coming from deep within the dark cavern.

"Harry!" Joel cried in relief. "Where are you?"

"Over here!" Harry called. "Hurry!"

Limping in the direction of his stepdad's voice, Joel

found him a few yards away, buried up to his neck in a pit of black goo. "What happened?" Joel gasped.

"Looks like we both fell into the same underground cavern," Harry said. "I wasn't hurt, so I decided to take a quick look around and stepped into this stuff. It looked solid when I stepped into it, but it sure sucked me down like quicksand."

"I'll go for help," Joel said.

"No, I think you can pull me out," Harry insisted. "The rope is still tied to my waist. Grab ahold of that frayed end and start tugging."

Joel found where the yellow nylon rope emerged from the black goo and pulled on it with all his might. But Harry didn't budge.

"Look, Harry. It's no use. I'm going for help," Joel said after a few more unsuccessful attempts.

"Okay, but hurry," Harry said, beginning to sweat. "Whatever this stuff is, it seems to be getting hotter."

For a moment Joel hesitated. "I don't know how long it'll take to find somebody," he said. "Will you—"

"Just go," Harry snapped. Then his face broke into a wide grin. "And you don't need to tell me to stay put."

Joel smiled at his stepdad. He could tell Harry was more frightened than he wanted to let on.

Ignoring the pain in his ankle, Joel rapidly scaled the incline to the path above. Emerging in the open, he took a deep breath of fresh air. A lot of the heavy mist had burned off and the sun was almost directly above him now. From his vantage point, he could see several miles in every direction. Shading his eyes, Joel looked for a sign of life but saw no one in sight.

Then he heard the distant whine of a chain saw and

turned to look in the direction of the sound. A few miles away he could see a group of forestry trucks gathered around a stand of pine trees.

"Harry!" he called, leaning into the crevice. "I see someone. Hang in there. I'll have you outta there in no time."

The path beneath his feet was covered with loose rocks, and Joel had trouble keeping his balance as he slid downhill toward the trucks. With his ankle hurting terribly, he still kept going until finally he'd reached the bottom of the trail . . . and that's when he heard it.

Beginning with a low rumble, deep in the bowels of the earth, the ground beneath Joel's feet began to tremble, then abruptly stopped. *Earthquake!* his mind screamed.

Frozen with terror, he waited for the aftershock, afraid to step in any direction. But before he could even think about moving, Joel heard a loud explosion, and the flat surface of the rock around him disintegrated before his eyes. Then, to his horror and amazement, a fountain of volcanic lava erupted beneath his feet.

For a second he thought he heard Harry—old Heart of Stone—scream. But Joel didn't have time to worry about the man, or even to worry about himself. All he had time to do was let out an ironic laugh as he thought the last thing he would ever think: *Too bad Harry won't be able to report back to my mom that I'm not afraid of earthquakes anymore,* Joel's tortured mind mused. *Now I'm afraid of volcanoes!*

THERE'S NO PLACE LIKE HOME

◊ ◊ ◊ ◊ ◊ ◊ ◊

The monster waddled closer. Its eyes glowed bright red as it entered the darkened nursery and looked around. The baby cooed happily in its crib. The monster heard the sound and started toward the child on short, scaly legs, its breath ruffling the infant's curls as it gave a bloodthirsty bark.

Elizabeth's mother called from the kitchen. "Beth! Turn that trash off."

"Aw, Mom," Beth protested, her eyes glued to the TV.

"You've been watching way too much of that junk," her mother said firmly. Crossing to the TV, she pushed the off button and the screen faded to black just as the monster's jaw opened to reveal a set of razor-sharp teeth.

"There's nothing else to do," Beth whined.

"Come help me in the kitchen," her mother suggested. "You can make some sugar cookies."

"Big deal," Beth muttered, rolling her eyes.

"Then go outside," her mother said. "It's too nice to stay indoors."

"It's hot out there," Beth objected.

"Why don't you ride your bike down to the store and get some ice cream for dessert?" her mother offered.

"Oh, all right," Beth said, heaving a sigh. "Can I rent a video, too?"

Her mother sighed back. "TV, videos—that's all you want to do. You need to get more exercise, honey. Why don't you play with your brothers?"

"Mom, I'm almost fourteen," Beth said, wrinkling her nose as if the idea of playing with her brothers actually smelled. "Besides, they always want to tie me up."

Her mother sighed again, then went to get her purse. "Fine, rent another video."

A few minutes later Beth stood in the carport surveying her bike. Enormous tumbleweed thorns protruded from both tires. "I hate this place," she muttered, kicking a flat tire. "Now I'll have to walk."

The family had come to live in the desert that June when Beth's father was transferred to an office outside of Palm Springs. They were living in a rental property on the outskirts of town until her parents found a house. Beth had begged to remain on the East Coast with her grandparents until school started, but her mother wanted to keep the family together. So here they were—in the hottest, driest, windiest, most barren place Beth had ever seen.

Leaving her useless bike to stand there on its pancake tires, Beth headed down the driveway. It was a short walk to the store, but the wind was blowing at near gale force, and Beth had trouble keeping her balance.

As tiny tornadoes of dust swirled around her ankles, a tumbleweed bounced into her path and hooked onto her jeans. She kicked at it, but it stuck, and when she tried to free herself, one of the sharp thorns pricked her.

"Ow!" she cried, jerking her hand back. A bright drop of blood sprang from her finger, and she automatically put it to her mouth. Sucking her wound, she looked up at the blue, windswept sky. "I'd do anything to get *out* of this place!" she shouted.

"Would you really?" a voice behind her asked.

Beth whirled around to see a girl her own age coming down the steps of the house she was about to pass.

"I'm Marcie, and I heard what you said," the girl told her. "Would you really do *anything* to get out of here?"

"Well . . ." Beth hesitated. She hadn't known anyone was listening. "Uh, why do you want to know?"

"You're the new girl from down the street," Marcie said by way of answer. "I saw the moving van a couple of weeks ago. You have two brothers and a cat, right?"

Beth grinned. "That's me, all right."

"And you hate this place," Marcie said. "That's pretty clear."

Beth laughed. "What was your first clue? Don't tell me that little outburst I had a minute ago gave me away!"

Marcie smiled. "You want to come inside?" she asked, pointing to her house.

Beth hesitated. Her mother was expecting her to come right back. "Okay," she said. "But just for a minute."

Marcie turned and led the way up the porch steps. "Let's go into the family room," she suggested. Then she led the way down the hall.

But the room that Marcie led Beth into was not like any family room she had ever seen. It was a small room, totally void of furniture except for a desk and a chair. All the curtains were drawn and the windows were sealed with aluminum foil. On top of the desk sat a small computer attached to a pair of strange-looking headphones. Marcie crossed to the desk and pressed a button, and the computer came to life as a series of lights flashed across the monitor. She turned to Beth.

"Have you ever heard of virtual reality?" she asked.

"Sure," Beth said uncertainly. "Uh, it's like when you interact with a fake world created by computers, right?"

"Kind of," Marcie said, "except this is better. It's my brother Eric's invention."

"Looks interesting," Beth said, picking up the headphones. "So where's your brother now?"

"I think he's in there," Marcie replied, pointing to the screen.

"What do you mean, *in* there?" Beth echoed. She was beginning to feel uneasy.

"I mean, *inside* the virtual reality game he created," Marcie explained. "That's what I wanted to talk to you about. You see, when I heard you say you'd do anything to get out of here, I thought maybe you could go in there. Then maybe you could help me find my brother, too."

Dropping the headphones, Beth backed toward the door. "No, thanks," she said, looking at Marcie like she was crazy.

"Wait!" Marcie pleaded. "Don't go. If you do this one little thing, I promise you'll never be bored again. I'll send you anywhere you want to go for the rest of your life. You just can't tell anybody until my brother gets his invention patented. Besides, going in to look for Eric would really be a lot of fun . . . don't you think?"

"If it would be so much fun," Beth asked suspiciously, "why not go yourself?"

"Somebody who knows how to run it has to stay on the

monitor at this end," Marcie said. "In case something goes wrong again."

"*Again?*" Beth echoed.

"The wind was blowing so hard when Eric was trying to transmit that there was a power surge," Marcie explained. "It knocked him off course, and I don't know exactly where he is. The only way to find him is to put the program on repeat. But I need someone to make the trip in a hurry, and there's no one else around." She looked at Beth with pleading eyes. "You said you'd do *anything* to get out of here—well, here's your chance."

Beth's mind started spinning. She wanted to take the challenge, but she was afraid. "What happens if something goes wrong while I'm in there?" she asked.

"It won't," Marcie said, handing Beth a plastic device the size of a deck of cards. "All you have to do is take this beeper with you so I can track your signal. When you locate Eric, press the button. Then I can home in on your location and bring you both back together." She grinned. "It's really no big deal, but time is running out. The repeat program only works for a short while after the initial journey, which was about an hour ago."

"And afterward you'll send me anyplace I want to go?" Beth asked.

Marcie nodded.

"And anytime I want to go?" Beth countered.

Marcie crossed her heart. "Word of honor," she said.

"Okay, then," Beth agreed. Ignoring the prickle of fear that made her heart beat faster, she shoved the homing beeper into her pocket. "Let's go for it."

Marcie gave her a hug. "Thanks," she said. "Now, sit at the desk and put on the headphones. I'll do the rest."

Beth did as she was told, then Marcie crossed to one wall and pulled back a drape, revealing a wall panel of electrical equipment. "Ready?" she asked.

"Wait!" Beth cried. "How will I know your brother?"

"He'll spot you in a minute," Marcie answered. "But you'll recognize him, anyway. We're twins."

The last thing Beth saw was Marcie waving good-bye and a blue electrical arc leaping toward her from the monitor. In the next instant she found herself aboard a boat—a steamer, judging from the vapor rising from the vessel's single smoke stack—and she was surrounded by people and cargo. There was a good deal of noise and confusion, and several people were speaking in a language Beth didn't understand.

"Oh, no," she groaned, looking around frantically. Judging from the tangle of tropical trees and vegetation that grew along the water's edge on both shores, Beth could tell that the boat was cruising down the middle of a jungle river. But exactly which jungle river, and on what continent, she couldn't begin to guess.

Suddenly she heard a sharp crack behind her, and Beth whirled around to see a group of men standing in the bow of the boat shooting rifles into the river. Quickly stepping to the ship's railing to have a look, Beth saw a bumpy, gray-green log floating on the surface of the water.

Another sharp report of a rifle sounded, and Beth saw blood spurt into the water as what she thought was a log turned into a crocodile. It raised an ugly snout and gave a terrifying roar.

Then a man standing behind her pointed upstream. "Piranha!" he screamed.

Squinting in the direction the man pointed, Beth saw a

struggling mass of silver fish in the muddy waters. They hung like a cloud just beneath the surface, stretching in a circle for several yards as they moved toward the shore. Then there was a bright flash of scales as the mass descended on the injured crocodile. Instantly the animal's body began to heave and buck under the onslaught.

As Beth turned away from the horrid sight, she saw a boy grinning at her. "Care for a swim?" he asked in perfect English. He extended his hand, took Beth's, and shook it. "I'm Eric," he said. "I suppose Marcie sent you." Leaning on the rail beside Beth, he stared at the muddy waters below. "How did you like the show?"

"It was horrible," Beth said, grimacing to emphasize her disgust. "Uh, I'm Beth. Where are we?"

"We're on the Piranha River in South America, and you can guess how it got its name. Piranha have an amazing sense of smell when it comes to blood, don't they? Even a drop drives them into a feeding frenzy."

Beth shuddered. "I'm beginning to think there are worse places to live than the desert."

"Yeah," Eric said. "There's no place like home. The problem is, I'm not ready to go back yet."

Beth stared. "You're kidding, right?"

"No," Eric said flatly. "There's something I have to do before we leave. It won't take long, and you can come with me if you want."

"What are you going to do?" Beth asked cautiously.

"See that man up there with the rifle?" Eric pointed toward the bow of the boat. "He promised to teach me how to shoot. I want to bag a croc before I leave."

"I don't have time for that," Beth said. "My mother's expecting me home. Besides, shooting animals is disgusting."

"Crocodiles are hardly helpless," Eric said. "Didn't you see those teeth? Come on, Beth. Be a good sport."

"No way," Beth said firmly, taking the beeper from her jeans pocket. "We're out of here." But before she could press the button, Eric grabbed her wrist.

"Give me that," he said. "This is *my* invention, and nobody's going to tell me when to come and go."

For a few moments they struggled in silence, then Beth managed to jerk her wrist from Eric's grip . . . but the control unit flew from her hand and over the side of the boat.

"Now see what you've done!" Beth cried.

"What *I've* done," Eric argued. "You're the one who tossed it overboard."

"There it goes," Beth said, pointing to the plastic control as it bobbed to the surface in the boat's wake.

"We have to get it," Eric said. Pushing past Beth, he ran toward the rear of the boat with Beth right behind him. When they reached the stern, Eric put one foot on the rail. "I see it," he said. "Come on. We have to be together when we go back."

"Wait!" Beth screamed. "The piranha will get you."

"I don't have a scratch on me," Eric said. "They won't even know I'm there." Eric sat straddling the top of the rail. "Make up your mind, Beth. Are you coming or not?"

Beth hesitated. Then Eric shrugged and leaped into the churning waters.

Her heart pounding, Beth didn't know what to do. She could go into the river with Eric, or she could stay aboard the ship and spend the rest of her life in South America with no friends and only a few dollars of American money. Then, when she saw that Eric had grabbed the beeper, her choice seemed clear. She clambered over the rail. "Hey,

71

Eric," she cried. "Wait for me!" And with that she plunged into the muddy waters.

As she hit the river and surfaced, a crew member saw her and started shouting wildly at her. Then Beth heard the frantic screams of all the passengers on deck as they ran to the stern to look overboard. Suddenly an avalanche of life preservers rained down around her head, and Beth heard the boat's engines grind to a halt.

"I'm fine!" Beth called back to the waving crowd. "Don't worry!" And then she saw a square-headed silvery fish appear below the surface of the water.

It was in that horrifying instant that Beth saw the puncture wound on her finger. It was red and swollen. And then she remembered the prick of the tumbleweed she'd gotten earlier . . . in the real world.

"Help!" she cried out in alarm.

But in the next second she felt the water around her begin to churn as the feeding frenzy began.

CRY WOLF

◆ ◀ ◆ ◀ ◆ ◀ ◆

Jeremy looked up to see his dog limping across the corral. "Here, Wolf," he called as he climbed off the fence rail. "Where've you been, boy? It's almost dinnertime."

Wolf, a crossbreed of uncertain origin, came slowly toward him, his head held low and his tail between his legs. Stopping a few paces away, he dropped to the ground with a whimper.

"What's the matter, boy? Are you sick?" Jeremy asked, squatting to feel the dog's nose. It felt hot and dry, and Jeremy saw that his paws were crusted with dried blood.

Alarmed, Jeremy ran to the barn, where he found his grandfather shoeing Strawberry, a roan-colored mare. Rushing through the open door, he startled the horse, who tried to pull her hoof away from Jeremy's grandfather.

"Hold on there, Strawberry," the elderly man said, quickly straightening up and taking hold of the mare's halter. Then he turned to face Jeremy. "You know better than to run up behind a horse like that!"

"It's Wolf, Grandpa!" Jeremy cried. "He's down in the corral and his paws are all bloody!"

"If Wolf made it back to the ranch, he can last until I get there," his grandfather growled. "Now, go stay with your dog, boy. I'll be along in a minute." And with that, he turned back to the mare.

Jeremy quietly left the barn. His grandfather had been acting grumpy with everyone lately. Even Grandma had noticed, and Jeremy could tell she was worried that something was wrong. Shrugging, he hurried to the corral. Wolf lay where Jeremy had left him, and his tail thumped a weak welcome as the boy approached.

"You crazy hound," Jeremy said, cradling the dog's head in his hands. "What have you been up to this time?"

Jeremy had come to live with his grandparents on their New Mexico ranch seven years ago when his parents died in a plane crash. The dog had wandered onto the ranch the same year, and although Jeremy was only six at the time, he'd convinced his grandparents that he would take care of the starving pup. Since then the orphan boy and the mongrel dog had been inseparable.

"Let's have a look at him," Jeremy's grandfather said, arriving with Manuel, the ranch foreman he'd hired a few months ago. Setting down a bucket, the old man squatted beside the dog, who suddenly growled.

"Wolf!" Jeremy cried. "Nobody's going to hurt you!"

"Can't take any chances," his grandfather said. Reaching in his pocket, he drew out a leash with a muzzle attached and quickly slipped it over Wolf's jaw. Then he carefully scooped water from the bucket to wash each of the dog's paws. "I don't see any cuts here," he said. "But we'd better keep him tied up in the barn to be safe."

Jeremy started to protest, but his grandfather raised his hand and stopped him.

"Now, don't start arguing!" he snapped. "Just go put your grandma's suitcase in the pickup—I'm taking her to Aunt Martha's. We'll talk about Wolf when I get back." And with Manuel at his side, he walked briskly to the barn, dragging Wolf at the end of the leash.

"And don't go worrying your grandmother over this, you hear?" he called over his shoulder. "She has enough on her mind as it is."

Jeremy's heart sank as he heard his grandfather's last words. Something was definitely wrong. Grandpa told Grandma everything.

After his grandparents had left, Jeremy went into the barn to check on Wolf. He found the dog fast asleep, tied to the feed bin in one of the empty horse stalls. Jeremy brought over some food and water, then removed the dog's muzzle, but Wolf still didn't get up.

In the next stall Strawberry stood dozing. The day was hot and Jeremy was also getting drowsy. Yawning, he stretched out on a bale of hay and decided to nap until Wolf woke up.

Three hours later Manuel was standing over him. "Hey, sleepyhead," he said. "Rosa made your favorite—chicken enchiladas. Your grandfather said to eat with us tonight."

"Thanks. I'll be there after I check on Wolf," Jeremy said. Groggily standing up, he stepped into the stall where he'd left the injured dog. He dropped to his knees and stroked Wolf's head. "I'll be back after I eat, fellow," he said softly. Then he ran out the barn door and down the dirt road to Manuel's house.

During dinner the phone rang, and Manuel's wife, Rosa, answered it. When she came back to the table, she looked extremely angry. "Vera told me of another killing," she told Manuel. "Why didn't you tell me?"

Manuel glanced toward Jeremy. "We'll talk later, Rosa," he said.

"No!" Rosa shouted. "We will talk now!"

Then, with a sinking heart, Jeremy learned that some kind of animal had been attacking livestock on the neighboring ranches for the past few months. The killings had started around the twenty-first of June—the night of the summer equinox—and had happened on or around the full moon every month afterward.

What had everyone most upset was that the slain animals had been ripped to shreds, but none of the flesh was eaten. Wild beasts will kill only for food, so people suspected a farm dog gone bad.

But Rosa had a different explanation. Leaning toward Jeremy, she whispered, "It's what you call a werewolf."

"Quiet, Rosa!" Manuel exclaimed. "Do you want to get me fired?"

Jeremy's eyes grew wide. "A werewolf!" he gasped.

"Don't listen to her, Jeremy," Manuel said. "Rosa is talking crazy."

"Hah!" Rosa said. "We'll see." And with that she went to the cabinet where Manuel kept his rifle. Unlocking the glass door, she returned with a box of ammunition and spilled the contents onto the kitchen table. Half a dozen silver cartridges lay among the rest.

Rosa turned to Manuel. "If you don't believe in werewolves, then why do you steal silver bullets from the boy's grandfather?"

Angrily Manuel scooped all of the bullets into his pocket. "You meddle in things you don't understand," he said shortly. Then he turned to Jeremy. "I'm sorry, boy. My wife and I have many things we need to discuss."

"Uh, sure," Jeremy said. "I'd better go."

As he hurried along the road toward home, Jeremy could hear Rosa and Manuel arguing. Above, a full moon lit the sky, but it held little interest for Jeremy. He didn't believe in werewolves, and although Rosa had startled him, he was more worried that Wolf was responsible for the killings. His grandfather probably suspected Wolf, too, and that's why he hadn't mentioned the killings. Suddenly a wave of sorrow engulfed Jeremy. If Wolf was the culprit, he'd have to be put down. There was nothing worse than a ranch dog gone bad.

As he neared the barn, Jeremy could hear Wolf inside, whining loudly and scratching on the stall door. Suddenly he had an idea. The bright moonlight made it easy to see. If he let Wolf out of the barn, he could follow him and prove the dog's innocence to his grandfather!

Crossing to the barn, Jeremy slipped inside, neglecting to secure the door behind him. He then took a flashlight from the wall and shone the beam directly into Wolf's stall. The dog was there, straining at the end of his leash. Jeremy hurried to him and unbuckled his collar. Then the boy dropped to his knees to hug him, but Wolf wriggled loose and ran past him and out the barn door.

Panicking, Jeremy ran after him, calling for the dog to stop. But Wolf would not obey, and Jeremy could see his silver coat gleaming in the moonlight as he galloped across the meadow and disappeared into a stand of cottonwood trees.

Down the road, Manuel stepped onto his porch and peered into the darkness. "What's wrong, Jeremy?" he called. "Is everything all right?"

Frozen to the spot, Jeremy didn't know what to do. It had never occurred to him that Wolf might run away.

"Answer me, Jeremy!" Manuel said sternly. "Do you need help?"

Then, as if things weren't bad enough, Jeremy saw his grandfather's truck coming down the road. If he found Wolf gone, he'd never let Jeremy follow the dog into the woods. Coming to a quick decision, Jeremy yelled back to Manuel that he was fine and that he'd see him tomorrow.

Manuel hesitated, shrugged, and went back into his house. Then, crouching low, Jeremy streaked across the meadow and into the woods after Wolf.

Although the moon was bright, Jeremy still had trouble seeing where he was going as he crashed through the thick underbrush. There was no path as such, and the floor of the forest was littered with fallen branches. Soon one of those branches caught his foot and sent him tumbling to the ground.

Trying to stand, Jeremy discovered his foot was trapped between two roots. As he sat there, wiggling his ankle back and forth in an effort to pry it loose, he heard the branches rustle nearby—as if someone or something were moving toward him through the forest. Then, abruptly, the noise stopped.

Jeremy held his breath. He could hear raspy breathing, but it was impossible to tell if the sound came from man or beast. But one thing Jeremy did know—whatever it was, it had stopped to listen, just as he was listening to it.

Terrified, he put his hand over his mouth to keep from crying out. Then, as abruptly as it had approached, whatever it was changed direction and moved away. Jeremy sat still for a few minutes, hardly daring to breathe, then he jerked his foot loose. Jumping to his feet, he ran headlong toward the meadow in the center of the woods, where he thought his dog would be.

Sure enough, as soon as he reached the edge of the clearing, he saw Wolf, the silver ruff around his neck outlined in the moonlight. Careful not to make a sound, Jeremy hid behind a tree to see what would happen next. He didn't have long to wait.

Jeremy whirled around to see a large creature coming toward him through the woods! Once again, he could hear its raspy wheeze as it lumbered through the underbrush. Sucking in his breath and hunkering down in hopes of shrinking out of sight, Jeremy froze in terror.

It was Strawberry!

With a groan, Jeremy remembered that he'd left the barn door open. Now he would have to take the frightened mare home. Letting his breath out in a long sigh, he got to his feet to catch her. And then Jeremy realized something that made him sick to his stomach.

The minute Wolf had seen Strawberry, he'd risen up on his haunches, and now he was creeping up behind the mare. As he watched the dog crouch and prepare to spring, Jeremy realized that Wolf was stalking the horse. Luckily a ranch dog couldn't bring down an animal that size alone, but it was now clear the dog had turned bad.

Selecting a sturdy cottonwood limb in case he was forced to defend Strawberry, Jeremy started off into the meadow. And then he saw it. There, on the other side of the clearing, lay *another* dog, partially hidden by the trees. As Jeremy watched, it rose and stepped out of the shadows into plain view.

Gasping, Jeremy found himself looking at a canine that

was bigger than any he had ever seen. Covered with dark, coarse hair, it growled, sending moonlight gleaming off its sharp white teeth.

Run! Jeremy's mind screamed as the creature dropped on its back and began to roll in the sweet grass of the meadow. But the boy was paralyzed, unable to think and too frightened to move.

Then Strawberry raised her head and whinnied, and Jeremy knew that she was afraid, too. He had to do something. Dropping to his knees, he began to slowly crawl toward the mare, praying that the creature wouldn't notice him in the tall grass.

But now the creature was up on all fours and creeping toward Strawberry. Panicked, Jeremy jumped to his feet. "Stop!" he yelled. "Get away from my grandfather's horse!"

Stopping in its tracks, the creature directed its gaze toward Jeremy, its eyes smoldering like hot coals.

"Get back," Jeremy warned as he walked toward Strawberry, the cottonwood branch raised in one hand. Then with the other he hit the mare hard on the rump. "Go home!" he shouted. And with that, Strawberry galloped out of the clearing.

With a low growl, the creature now began to move toward Jeremy with long, measured strides.

Then, before Jeremy had a chance to think, the animal leaped through the air and knocked him to the ground with one powerful lunge. Standing over the trembling boy, its lips curled back, the creature revealed itself as the terrible being that it was—a werewolf!

Sure his life was over, Jeremy was about to let out one last scream when suddenly he saw surprise reflected in the creature's eyes. Then, all at once, Wolf flew at the beast, locking his teeth into the werewolf's throat.

Roaring with fury, the werewolf tossed its mighty head with such power that Wolf went flying halfway across the clearing. The faithful dog fell with a thud and just lay there, stunned.

Seeing his chance, Jeremy leaped to his feet, grabbed the cottonwood branch, and brought the heavy limb down hard across the werewolf's back. "Run, Wolf!" Jeremy screeched. "Run home!"

But Wolf was not about to leave his master. As the creature turned on Jeremy, the dog renewed his attack from behind. He locked his teeth into the werewolf's ear, and the creature howled with pain. Tossing its massive head, once again it sent Wolf through the air—this time into the trees.

Jeremy heard a thud as the dog's body connected with a tree trunk. Then there was silence.

Furious over what the werewolf had done to Wolf, Jeremy now faced the beast bravely, gripping his cottonwood club with all his might. But with a single lunge, the creature tore the branch from the boy's grasp, snapping the limb in half with its mighty jaws.

His weapon destroyed, Jeremy turned and ran with the creature in hot pursuit. But it was an uneven match. The werewolf's powerful legs brought him upon Jeremy in mere seconds, knocking the boy to the ground. Feeling the hot moisture of the terrible beast's breath on the back of his neck, Jeremy braced himself for what he was sure would be the end . . . and then a shot rang out.

Howling in pain, the werewolf fell off Jeremy's body and went crashing to the ground. Stunned, Jeremy sat up and gazed into the anxious face of his grandfather.

"Are you hurt, boy?" his grandfather asked.

Jeremy's arm was bleeding, but otherwise he seemed unharmed. Unconsciously sucking at the wound, Jeremy looked around. "Grandpa, where's Wolf?" he asked frantically. "He saved my life!"

His grandfather smiled and pointed to the brave dog, now limping over. "You're okay, fellow!" Jeremy gasped with relief as he threw his arms around Wolf. And then, as if in answer, Wolf licked Jeremy's hand.

"Let's go home, boy. Let's—" Jeremy stopped and looked around. "Grandpa?" he called. "Where'd you go?"

"Over here, son," his grandfather called back.

Jeremy dragged himself to his feet and limped over to his grandfather, who was bending over the werewolf on the ground. The beast lay on its back, a single bullet hole above its heart. Then, as Jeremy and his grandfather watched, the creature began to change its form right before their eyes. There, in the bright moonlight, Jeremy saw the hairy body shiver and convulse as it became the figure of a man.

"Manuel!" Jeremy exclaimed. "But—but he had silver bullets to hunt the werewolf. And Rosa said . . ." Stunned, Jeremy couldn't go on.

His grandfather shook his head. "I wondered where my bullets went," he said. "Well, it's all over now. Let's go home, Jeremy. We'll think up some story so we can give Manuel a proper burial. But not a word of what really happened tonight, you hear?"

Jeremy nodded solemnly. Then he whistled for Wolf and they all headed for home.

As he walked across the meadow with his grandfather, Jeremy looked down at the scrape on his arm. The blood had dried, and it didn't hurt at all. In fact, the gentle breeze felt like a feather on his skin. And although everything felt fine and he and Wolf were safe, Jeremy couldn't help wondering why he suddenly felt the strongest urge to howl at the large full moon above.

MY FATHER, THE V.P.

◇ ◇ ◇ ◇ ◇ ◇ ◇

The day before my thirteenth birthday, I noticed that my right eyetooth was growing. I was combing my hair in front of the hall mirror when I saw it, and I put on my glasses to take a better look.

"Anything new, Carl?" my father murmured, pausing on the stairs.

I was up before dawn that morning, on my way to football practice, and my dad was on his way to bed. You see, he worked nights, and we saw each other only on the rare occasions that we happened to meet in the hall.

I turned to face him. He met my look, and I lowered my eyes as he waited for an answer to his question. "Nothing's new," I said.

I wasn't about to discuss the length of my tooth with my father—or anything else. It wasn't that we didn't get along, exactly. We just never did anything together. It was just as well, since my father always made me feel like I was from another planet. And I *knew* he was!

"By the way," Dad said. "It's time you learned about the family line of work. Keep tomorrow night free." He started up the stairs to his bedroom on the second floor.

I stared at him open-mouthed. "You want me to go to work with you tomorrow night?" I asked.

"That's right," he said. "You look surprised."

Surprised! I was astonished. "But it's my birthday," I managed to croak out.

"What better way to celebrate?" my father said, pausing on the third step. "Sure there's nothing new with you?" he asked again.

I shook my head silently.

My father shrugged and continued up the stairs. "See you later," he said over his shoulder.

"Yeah, see you later," I mumbled under my breath as I walked into the kitchen.

"Did your father remember to tell you about tomorrow night?" my mom asked as soon as I sat down at the table.

I nodded. To my way of thinking, my mother led a strange sort of life. Right after she fed my dad dinner every morning, she fixed breakfast for me. Weird, huh?

"Why doesn't Dad ever work the day shift?" I asked.

My mom looked at me. "Your father has a very important position in the family business," she said.

"Yeah, sure," I muttered. "Night watchmen are the most important men around."

"Don't be silly, dear. Your father's the executive V.P.," my mother said in a firm tone.

"V.P.? Like in vice president?" I asked sarcastically.

"Of course," my mother said. "Now, eat your steak and eggs. You'll be late for your football practice."

I bit into my steak. It was rare, just the way I liked it. But my long tooth felt funny as I chewed, and I ended up leaving half the meat on my plate when I ran out the door, late as usual.

We had a hard practice, and I pretty much forgot about my tooth until I was showering in the junior high school gym. That's when my friend John asked if I'd been hit in the face or something during a tackle.

"Not that I can remember," I answered. "I took some pretty good hits, but my face feels fine."

"So where'd you get that lump?" John asked, pointing to the left side of my jaw.

I felt my lip. It was warm, and I could feel it pulsing—like something was about to erupt underneath. It scared me.

What's happening to my body? I wondered. Worried, I rushed into the bathroom to look in the mirror. It was clouded with steam, and without my glasses, I had trouble making out my image. I sighed. I would be thirteen the following day, and I still looked like a little kid. No beard. No muscles. No fair! Groaning at my cloudy image, I wondered if I was ever going to get any bigger.

Leaning toward the mirror, I pulled my lip back and examined my eyeteeth. The gum around the left one looked red and swollen, and the tooth on the right appeared to be even longer than it had been earlier.

"At least *some*thing's growing," I said, chuckling at my reflection. Then I remembered seeing a photograph of my mother when she was about my age. She had braces on her teeth in the picture, and I decided that my teeth were probably just like hers—in need of correction. Sure that I'd figured it all out, I put my sore eyeteeth out of my mind, hurriedly got dressed, and ran to class.

But as soon as I got home from school that day, I went straight to my room and closed the door so I could think.

Two things still weren't making any sense. My eyeteeth were clearly growing way out of proportion to the rest of my teeth, and my father was taking me to work with him for my thirteenth birthday. On the surface, these seemed like two totally unrelated happenings. But were they? It made me wonder.

My father's job had always been something of a mystery to me. He had worked nights as long as I could remember, a situation that my mother seemed to accept in spite of the fact that it allowed her very little social life. I had never known exactly what Dad did. All I knew was that he called it "the family business." Still, if he was really an important V.P., as my mother claimed, why did he have to work nights? I just assumed he was a night watchman. After all, what kind of business operated after dark?

I remained in my room all afternoon trying to fit the pieces of the puzzle together. The solution still eluded me all the way into the early evening, when I heard the door to my father's room open. Then I heard his footsteps in the hall, and I knew he would be going to work as soon as the sun set.

That's when I got an idea. There was no reason to wait until my thirteenth birthday to find out the answers to all my questions. I could follow my father to work that very night and learn right away what all the mystery was about. I was going to find out soon enough, anyway, and besides, I wanted—no, I *needed*—to know.

It was dark outside by the time my father left the house.

I had told my mom that I was going to the library to work on a paper, but instead I went out the back door and hid behind a tall hedge, waiting for my dad to pass in front of me.

Sure enough, my father came by right on schedule—six-thirty. His office was in downtown Chicago, and he always took the six-thirty commuter train to work during the winter months. In summer, he left somewhat later. I had never wondered why his schedule changed during the warmer months, but now that I was beginning to examine his behavior for clues, I realized that it was still light at six-thirty that time of the year.

At a safe distance, I followed him the two miles to the train station. My father always walked there—even when it snowed—and he was in such good shape I had to trot to keep up with his long strides. We reached the station at the same time as the train, and my dad swung on board while I hurried to buy a ticket. I had barely enough time to find a seat in the last car before the train pulled out of the station, bound for the city.

The trip was long and uneventful. I could see my father in the car ahead, but I stayed glued to the window so if he got off the train before we reached the station, I'd spot him and be able to follow.

But he didn't get off the train until it pulled into downtown—just as I'd expected.

The station was crowded with commuters. In a way I was glad it was crowded because it helped me hide from my father. But at one point I thought I'd lost him, and in an effort to keep an eye on him, I practically knocked down this poor elderly woman. For a moment I debated whether to just leave her with her packages sprawled out all over the floor, but I knew I couldn't do that. So by the time I had finished helping her pick up all her stuff and had apologized like crazy, my dad had disappeared.

I stood gazing around, puzzled. I was about to give up, when he showed up again with the evening paper in his hand. Walking briskly, he headed up the stairs and out a side door. In a flash I was after him.

The side door he had taken opened out onto a busy street choked with traffic. My father turned down a side alley, and soon our footsteps echoed along deserted sidewalks. The tall office buildings on either side were closed for the night, their lobbies empty.

I followed at a short distance behind him for several blocks. Then my father paused under a corner street lamp and looked back in my direction.

Springing into the nearby alley, I pressed my back against a cold brick wall. *Had he seen me?* I wondered, my heart beating so loudly against my rib cage I was sure he would hear.

Then I heard his footsteps resume. After a few moments I started to step out onto the sidewalk to resume tailing him, when suddenly a hand gripped my shoulder from behind!

"Are you lost, little boy?" a voice said in my ear.

I struggled in an effort to free myself, but the man's strong grip tightened. He stepped out of the shadow and I saw his face. It was creased with age, his skin as scuffed and battered as the leather on my old football.

He towered over me, a good six feet in height. Then he leaned down and the folds of his black cape brushed the ground where I stood. His eyes burned into mine—holding me captive, pinning me to the spot where I stood. As he bent toward me, he smiled, and his lips pulled back to reveal two long fangs.

Without thinking, I smiled back, about to make some stupid joke about a vampire, when my lip got hung up on my right eyetooth. At the same time I could feel my left fang beginning to throb. I must have looked really weird

with this geeky crooked smile on my face.

Anyway, the vampire looked at me kind of startled. He took a step backward, at the same time loosening his hold on my shoulder. Seeing my chance, I wriggled out of his grasp and pushed him with all my strength.

"Leave me alone!" I yelled, breaking free and running out of the alley onto the sidewalk.

"Wait!" he called, coming after me. "You don't understand!"

But I didn't stop for an explanation. I ran as fast as I could, my footsteps echoing along the empty sidewalks. Stopping to catch my breath, I stood under the same street lamp that my dad had paused under a few minutes before.

Suddenly the sound of footsteps on the pavement behind me told me that someone was nearing the corner at the other end of the block. It was probably that guy who'd just grabbed me. As he came closer, I could hear him wheeze every time he drew a breath. I looked around frantically, looking for a place to hide.

Then I saw it.

There was a light coming from a window in the building across the street, and I could see the silhouette of a figure moving inside. I hesitated, not really knowing what to do. I had lost sight of my father, but it stood to reason he had gone up into the only room on the block that showed any kind of light. Even if he wasn't there, maybe there was somebody there I could ask for help. On the other hand, if my father was in that room, it would mean I'd have to explain to him why I was there.

As I stood there, debating with myself, I heard the ever-approaching footsteps, now only yards away. The lighted room seemed to be my only chance.

Running for it, I heard my pursuer hot on my heels as I dashed into the building and across the empty lobby and up a staircase.

"Wait!" the man called. "I need to talk to you."

Talk to me? Who was he trying to kid?

I came out of the stairwell onto the second floor and raced down the hall toward an open doorway filled with light.

Panting, I dashed through the door, then skidded to a stop. The room was full of people sitting in rows of chairs. The banner across the front of the room read: V.A. INCORPORATED. On a side wall a sign read: "Does your life suck? Call the V.A. Hotline for help. Lines open every night after dark." On another wall, a sign read: "Learn the 12 Steps to Personal Freedom."

I looked around in puzzlement.

My father stood at the front with his back to the room. He finished writing something on a blackboard before he turned to face the group. When he saw me, he smiled.

"Carl!" he exclaimed, not looking upset to see me at all. "I thought that boy following me looked a lot like you." He turned to the group. "Everyone, this is my son. Tomorrow is his thirteenth birthday, but obviously he couldn't wait to join us."

A ripple of laughter spread through the room as over fifty pairs of eyes looked in my direction. Then the man who had been chasing me rushed through the door.

"Help!" I yelped, charging to the other side of the room. "That man is after me!"

My father's expression changed from that of welcome to one of mild reproach. "Hello, Henry," he said. "Been up to your old tricks again, have you?"

Henry looked embarrassed. "I'm sorry," he said, gazing around the room. "I didn't know the boy was one of us when I spoke to him."

My mouth dropped open. "One of us?" I managed to say. "What does he mean by *us*?"

"Henry is a member of our family," my dad said. He turned to Henry. "Okay, Henry. It's time to tell the group who you are."

"Hello, everybody," the man said. "My name's Henry and I'm a vampire."

I looked around, waiting for someone to scream or call the police. But everyone just sat there.

"Hello, Henry," the group echoed.

A woman smiled, her lips curling back from a set of shiny braces. She reminded me of my mom.

"Oh, no," I groaned as reality began to dawn on me.

I looked at my dad. He was smiling at me. "It's your turn, Carl."

"My turn?" I echoed. *What does he mean, my turn?* my mind screamed in confusion.

"I planned to bring you here to V.A. tomorrow night, just as my father brought me on my thirteenth birthday," my dad explained. "But it doesn't matter. I'm glad you're here tonight. There's so much I haven't been able to share with you, Carl. And now I can." He smiled and revealed two long fangs just like the man who had chased me. "There's no reason why you can't make your choice one day earlier, son. If you decide to dedicate your life to helping others like yourself, you can become part of the family business right here tonight."

My head was spinning. What was my father talking about? "Uh, Dad, wouldn't this be a good time to tell me just what *is* the family business?" I asked stupidly. "I mean, what does V.A. stand for, anyway?"

"Why, Vampires Anonymous," my father said, frowning. "I thought you'd have figured it out by now. We're devoted to helping other vampires wean themselves off human blood and onto that of smaller animals like—"

"Uh, that's okay, Dad. I get the picture," I said, looking around in a daze. The room was silent. I saw all the upturned, smiling faces around me . . . and *lots* of eyeteeth gleaming in the light. Then it suddenly became clear. I was in a room full of vampires. My *father* was a vampire. Probably my *mother* was a vampire. And that only meant that . . .

Suddenly I could feel my two canine teeth tingling as I stood there, trying to take it all in. I saw my father looking at me expectantly, and I knew what I had to do. I turned to face the group.

"Hello, everyone," I said. "My name's Carl, and I'm a vampire, too."

FOR OTHER

TIMELY TERRORS,

READ . . .

Three-Minute Thrillers
More Three-Minute Thrillers

Six-Minute Mysteries

More Six-Minute Mysteries